INFESTATION

CHRIS
SHEEHAN

INFESTATION

ISBN: 978-0-9937931-0-3

www.ChrisSheehan.ca

*To my loving parents
for all their support*

Chapter 1

"Be careful with those! They're antiques!"

That would be my mother yelling at one of the movers again. She's standing by the curb, next to the moving truck, ordering them around like little children or something. I watch as she grabs the so-called antique lamps from them, which she bought brand new three years ago I might add, and sets off towards the house. Appearances are everything to her; she always has to look like she has it all.

After everything that's happened, I guess I shouldn't be too hard on her. When my father decided to leave us last year it hit her pretty hard. She has always put on a strong front but I know she is hurting on the inside. I mean they were together for years and then one day he just decides to leave us for his blonde, big breasted, dumb as a post secretary. Yeah, I'm still mad at him. Who wouldn't be?

After the divorce, Mom decided we needed a change of scenery and chose to move us to the little, old town of Crescent Falls. A small community surrounded by fields on all sides. I can understand her reasoning; but at the same time, I'm kind of pissed at the timing of it all.

This is going to be my senior year of high school and my birthday is in a week. All my friends are back in New York and now we are in the middle of NOWHERE! Couldn't this have waited a year?

"Lily! Stop daydreaming. Get out of the car and help." My mother calls to me as she passes the car on her way back to the truck. She's determined to make the movers cry at some point, I'm sure.

"I'll be right there." I reply as I take off the seat belt.

Stepping out of the vehicle, I finally get a full view of the house; it's huge. I've seen the pictures of course, but nothing compares to seeing it up close and in person. It's a luxurious two-story home with a gray stone and brick exterior. A stone walkway leads to a covered porch surrounded by gardens containing flowers of all colors. This is definitely an improvement over our cramped New York apartment. There is even a tan colored welcome mat lying just before the wooden front door. I guess we are home.

"At least we got some decent weather for this."

I nearly jump out of my skin, spinning around in the process. As I had been admiring the house before me, one of the movers had come to a stop at my side. He's carrying a couple boxes in his strong, muscular arms. A smirk appears on his face as he notices me staring at the biceps bulging beneath his tight shirt. My face starts to burn up in embarrassment as he walks towards the house laughing.

"Here, take this box to the kitchen." My mother, now standing by my side, passes me a decent sized box with the word KITCHEN scrawled across it. She then turns and hurries back to the truck while I head towards the house, determined to find the kitchen. As I approach the porch I can hear her yelling the word fragile. The young, buff mover from before decides to exit as I'm about to enter and my eyes immediately hit the floor. Keeping my head down I quickly move past him.

Boxes line the walls of the main foyer, piled three to four high. There is a wooden staircase leading to the second floor, a dining room with sliding glass doors to the left and an archway to the right opens onto a bright living room. Straight ahead, past the stairs, appears to be the kitchen. Well that wasn't very hard to find after all.

Stainless steel appliances, marble countertops, an island with room for at least five people to sit around, tile flooring, and lots of light... beautiful. A pair of French doors opens onto a wide open deck overlooking an enormous back yard. There is an in-ground pool, complete with diving board and even a hot tub at the far end of the deck. After placing the box on the island I decide to spend some time just taking it all in.

"So, what do you think?" My mother is standing in the doorway watching me.

"It'll do." I try to sound indifferent but the beaming smile smeared across my face gives me away. The corners of my mother's mouth turn up in a tiny grin as she enters the kitchen and leans against the counter.

"Listen, Lily. I know you're upset about having to leave your friends back in New York and having to move here before your final year, but I think this is the best thing for us right now. Besides, your friends can visit whenever they want and you'll make new ones here in no time."

"Yeah... It just really sucks."

"I know."

Is she referring to the move or the divorce I wonder, as she stands there with a distant look in her eyes. Deciding that this move might actually turn out to be a good thing, I walk over and wrap my arms around my mother. The long overdue and much needed hug lasts a few moments. A tear escapes and rolls down my mother's cheek.

"OK, let's get this move over with." She says, clearing her throat. "Most of your stuff is already in your room but there are a couple of boxes by the front door. Can you take them up? Remember, first door on the left."

With a smile on her face she leaves the room, heading back outside. Standing alone again in the kitchen, I call jokingly after her. "Don't be too hard on them!"

Back in the foyer, I pick up the first box with my name scribbled on it and head up the stairs, taking them two at a time. Turning left, I stop in front of the first closed door. Box in one hand, doorknob in the other, I slowly open the door and... SCREAM!

Chapter 2

The box crashes to the floor with a loud bang. In the middle of the room lies the largest, greenest, ugliest snake ever. How did a snake get into my room in the first place? It's just lying there, looking at me with those small, beady eyes as if it's staring into my soul. When it starts to move across the floor I let out another shriek and leap backwards. The closet on the other side of the room is apparently its target.

Grabbing the nearest weapon available, a tennis racket, I try to sneak up behind it. That's when I notice how the sunlight from the far window shimmers off of what looks to be fishing line wrapped around the snake's head. Wait a minute, it's not slithering at all but instead is slowly being dragged across the floor. I whack it with the racket and realize it's not even real; the snake is made of rubber.

Laughter erupts from behind the closet door, which I now notice is slightly ajar. Tossing the racket aside, I rush over and, kicking the rubber snake out of the way, burst into the closet. As I thought. My eleven year old brother is lying on his side, laughing so hard that his face is red and tears are flowing.

"Brandon! Stop laughing! It isn't funny!" I yell, resisting the urge to literally kick him while he's down, deciding to bide my time and get back at him later. After all, they do say that revenge is a dish best served cold.

"Oh my god, you thought it was real!" He manages to stand up and then begins mimicking me, swinging the racket around.

"Is everything OK up there? I heard screaming." My mother calls to us from the bottom of the stairs. Brandon is still swinging the racket around and playing with the damn rubber snake when I leave, making my way to my worried mother. The wave of relief is obvious on her face as I appear at the top of the stairs.

"Just Brandon being a jerk again." I say, as if that should explain everything.

"Can't you two just get along? Just for today? That's all I ask." She doesn't wait for me to reply but instead simply shakes her head and walks away.

When I head back outside, the truck is closed and the movers are talking to my mother. A wink is sent my way from the young mover as I approach, causing my temperature to rise ever so slightly. Money passes hands and thanks are said before the two men hop in their truck and drive off.

As we turn to go back inside, we both notice a woman and child heading our way across the lawn. The woman looks to be about forty years old, give or take. Her wavy, golden-brown hair flows behind her, grazing a baggy white t-shirt spotted with paint. The young boy appears to be around Brandon's age and none too thrilled about being dragged along. He walks with his arms crossed over a red t-shirt with a large image of an anthropomorphic turtle wielding nunchucks.

"Hi, my name's Mary and this little monster here is my son Devon." She places her hand on the top of Devon's head, ruffling his hair. The way Devon rolls his eyes is priceless. "We live next door."

"Nice to meet you. I'm Kate Cra... I mean Stewart and this is Lily, my daughter." My mother greets them, shaking hands with Mary. Since the divorce, my mother has gone back to using her maiden name, but sometimes she slips up. My brother and I have our father's last name of Crawford which can make things a little confusing sometimes. "I also have a son, Brandon, around here somewhere."

As if on cue, Brandon comes barging out the front door like a maniac, still carrying the tennis racket.

"Brandon, come over here and meet your neighbors." My mother beckons to him.

Bounding enthusiastically down the stairs of the porch, he races across the yard and comes to a halt in front of Devon.

"Hi, I'm Brandon." He drops the racket at his feet and sticks out his hand. "Wanna see my room?"

The two of them shake hands while Devon proceeds to give a very animated nodding of his head. For some reason I think he just wants to get away from his mother. They head off towards the house talking quietly. Before entering, they both turn around and, looking at me, burst out laughing. It fades as they disappear inside. Great, just what I need right now, another Brandon.

My mother invites Mary inside for some of the refreshing iced tea we brought with us and, after finding a few glasses, the three of us end up standing around the island talking. We find out that Mary is a teacher at the local public school and her husband Sam is the chief of police at the Crescent Falls police department.

After a while we decide to move our little gathering to the deck overlooking the backyard, bringing our glasses with us. Mary asks about my father at one point which causes my mother to choke up slightly and spill some of her drink. She holds it together pretty well though, explaining the divorce and how he ran off with his "slutty secretary". Her words not mine. Mary is quite understanding and casually changes the topic to me. How do I like the new house? Am I happy to be graduating this year? "It's great" and "obviously" are the answers I give. Somehow my birthday even comes up and the two of them spend what seems like an hour discussing party plans, allowing me to give a little input here and there.

The sun is beginning to set when Mary decides it is time to leave. We are all gathered in the foyer when she calls Devon to come down. Both boys appear at the top of the stairs, grinning from ear to ear.

"Time to go." Mary says. "You'll see Brandon tomorrow. You're in the same class."

"Sweet!" Both Brandon and Devon shout, almost in sync.

We say our goodbyes and wave as they cross the yard again, Devon racing off ahead.

"Lily, can you wash those glasses for me?" My mother asks once we are back inside. "I'm going to start unpacking."

I enter the kitchen, prepared to clean them when I remember they are still outside. While passing through the French doors to collect the glasses, I notice a couple red ants gathered around the spot of iced tea my mother had spilt earlier. Determined to get rid of them all, I raise my shoe high and bring it down hard, crushing them with a pop.

Chapter 3

"**O**h your biceps are so big." I say as the young mover stands topless before me, his blonde hair blowing in the cool breeze from across the ocean. We are in a clearing on the edge of a grass covered cliff, overlooking the crystal blue water. As I lightly kiss his strong, muscular arms, making my way to his smooth chiseled chest, he gently undoes the back of my billowing gown. It slowly falls to the ground as our lips lock and we embrace each other passionately. Holding me in his arms, he lays me on the soft earth and with the grass beneath me he starts to...

BEEP! BEEP! BEEP! BEEP!

The loud alarm on my phone rudely wakes me from the wonderful dream. Lazily reaching over to my nightstand, I fumble with the phone for a minute before eventually shutting it off. Bright, warm sunlight shines through a crack in the curtains, streaming across my face, causing me to squint. Groggily rubbing my eyes, I roll out from under the comforter and manage to make my way towards the bedroom door. Opening it, I see Brandon race into the washroom down the hall and slam the door behind him. DAMN!

"Hurry up, Brandon!" I shout, receiving no reply.

Most of the night had been spent unpacking and gradually getting my room in order. After slowly emptying box after box and organizing things to my liking, I was extremely exhausted and ended up passing out around one in the morning. Now, with only about five hours of sleep, I have to make it through the dreaded first day of school.

Brandon finally exits the much needed washroom and takes off down the stairs, allowing me to rush in and get myself ready. After a warm, relaxing shower, I sit alone in front of my bedroom mirror. Wearing only my robe, I begin brushing my hair and wonder what this new small-town school will be like. Back in New York, the school was huge and there were so many people that my friends and I were practically invisible. Being kind of tomboyish, I never had any interest in cheerleading or wearing heels and shopping like a lot of the so-called popular girls. And if you weren't popular, you weren't important. Will people like me? This thought crosses my mind while staring at my reflection. Will I like them? I put the brush down and get dressed.

Brandon is in the living room noisily slurping milk from a large bowl while lounging on the couch and watching some animated show on the flat screen. Heading into the kitchen, I find my mother, still in her pink pajamas, unpacking boxes and filling cupboards with dishes. A white bowl and silver spoon sit on the island and cereal boxes line the counter in front of a bubbling kettle.

"There's a bowl and cereal for you." My mother turns my way. "Milk's in the fridge." She motions towards the refrigerator while gently placing the last plate in the cupboard. Tossing the empty box aside and grabbing a mug, she makes her inviting morning coffee. I grab another mug and make one for myself. I have to get through this day somehow. Bowl in hand, I fill it with a store brand cereal, cover that with milk from the practically empty fridge and then find a spot at the island. My mother, fresh coffee in hand, takes a seat next to me.

"So I figured I would drop you and Brandon off at school before heading to the hospital." She says, laying out her plans while sipping her coffee. "Then I thought I would pick up some more groceries on the way home."

My mother is going to be the new hot-shot surgeon at Crescent Falls General. This will be her first day too. I imagine that she must be pretty nervous herself, not that she'd ever show it. Her work is her passion which means that when we were living in New York, Brandon and I had a lot of alone time. Sure, with my mother being a surgeon and our father being a busy dentist we always had plenty of money and the best of everything. However, it would have been nice to have both of my parents around once in a while. Now that she is going to be one of the only surgeons in this small town, that alone time is probably only going to increase. As happy as I am for her, I still wish she was home more often.

"Sounds good to me." I jokingly reply in between bites. "Food would be nice."

With a smile and a nod my mother casually stands up, rinses her now empty mug and places it in the dishwasher. Brandon comes rushing into the kitchen, tosses his bowl and spoon in the sink and then takes off back to the living room. The show must have been on commercial. My mother looks up at the ceiling and lets out a loud sigh before rinsing his bowl as well. After placing it in the dishwasher she goes to leave.

"I've got to go get ready." She motions to a couple boxes along the wall. "Can you do me a favor and take those to the basement?"

Chapter 4

With one of the boxes in hand, I open the basement door which leads under the stairs to the second floor. It may be hard to believe, but this is my first time actually entering a basement. The adrenaline starts to surge through me as my excitement grows. Being born and raised in New York and growing up in a fifth floor apartment, we never had a basement. Sure there were underground parking garages and the subway, but they just don't compare.

As I start to carefully descend the creaky stairs, my face is attacked by numerous cobwebs. Startled and dropping the box, which tumbles to the bottom of the dark stairs, I frantically begin swiping at the webs covering me. Maybe this won't be such a great experience after all. The webs are clinging to my hair and spread across my face. How utterly disgusting!

After making sure that every last horrible strand has been removed, I finally find the light switch and flip it on. The narrow staircase I am currently frozen on is bordered on both sides by plywood walls. There doesn't appear to be any more webs hanging across my path and thankfully there are no spiders in sight. A chill runs through me as I picture my face knocking them all down.

The basement itself is large but unfinished and certainly doesn't meet the caliber of the rest of the house. With a floor made of cold cement and nothing covering the concrete block outer walls, a wave of disappointment washes over me. Reaching the bottom of the staircase I collect the now dented box and quickly stuff all the plastic Christmas ornaments back in.

I take a brief look around while figuring out where to leave the troublesome box. Many small windows, which let in a minimal amount of light, are positioned around the basement. A couple are actually smashed and sharp shards of glass lay beneath them. There is a wide laundry room easily seen as the walls are composed of only a wooden frame. Within, a high capacity washer and dryer stand beside a deep wash tub. Next to that is the only room with finished walls and a door which sits slightly ajar. Probably just a washroom, I think to myself. An old looking, somewhat menacing, furnace sits against the far wall. The back area of the basement opens onto a large space, most likely meant to be a rec room of sorts.

Feeling that it is the best place to leave the box, I casually make my way towards the back of the musty basement. That is when the horrible smell hits me, assaulting my nostrils and almost knocking me to my knees. The putrid stench seems to be flowing out of the closed off room. It is like meat that has been left rotting in the sun for weeks while coated in spoiled milk. I can't help but gag as my breakfast tries to make a triumphant return.

With my nose completely covered by one hand, I rush past. I leave the box in the open space at the back before returning to the dreadful room. Intent on finding the source of the foul odor, I use my free hand to fully open the squeaky door. Thousands of black flies burst forth, causing me to scream out and drop to the floor. I cower, covering my face, waiting for it to end.

They buzz all around me as I lay there trembling with my hands over my head. I can feel their prickly little legs crawling over my bare hands, through my hair and even inside my shirt. One starts making its way up the leg of my pants while another couple get entangled in my long hair and start violently thrashing about. As I let out another loud shriek, one even manages to enter my open mouth and crawls along my tongue. Its wings brush softly, like a feather, against the top of my mouth while it continues towards the back of my throat. After quickly spitting it out and feeling the urge to vomit, one more howl erupts from me.

I suddenly hear movement on the floor above me. Somebody must have heard my terrified wails.

"Lily? What's wrong?" My mother charges down the basement stairs. "Are you OK?" She comes to an abrupt halt a few feet away. I hear her gasp. "Oh my goodness." She whispers under her breath, but loud enough for me to hear.

"Mom, help me!" I scream, trying not to open my mouth too wide.

She is now kneeling by my side trying her best to swat away the flies. Her eyes are wide as she gently pulls me to my feet and helps me away from the room. Multiple flies tumble from my pant legs and a few shoot out from inside my shirt. As my mother tries to comfort me, I notice Brandon standing by the stairs watching with a look of shock and amazement.

After explaining what happened and plucking every last fly from my hair, we begin opening windows with the hope that they will find their way outside. They head in different directions with the majority leaving through the broken glass of the side windows. Once the area has somewhat cleared around what we can now tell for sure is a washroom, Brandon moves over to get a better look. He lets out a sound of disgust as he enters.

"Ewww... Man that's gross." Brandon exclaims, leaving the washroom with his nose covered.

Passing us hurriedly, he heads back upstairs while my mother and I cautiously check it out together. With my mother's arm around my shoulder, we both plug our noses and peek into the washroom. A grotesque sight awaits us. In the middle of the cold floor lies what could have been a young possum. The body has rotted away to the point that it is hard to make out what it used to be. There are multiple open wounds including the animal's stomach which appears to have burst open. The remaining fur is matted and caked with blood which has also dried in a puddle around the body. Numerous maggots crawl on and inside the corpse, devouring what is left of it. I see them worming their way through the gaping wounds and within the sunken eye sockets. Unable to hold back any longer, I let forth my breakfast all over the cement floor.

My mother continues to hold my hair back until my stomach has emptied and I give way to dry heaving. After repeatedly reassuring her that I will be fine alone, she leaves and returns moments later with a garbage bag, towels and a dust pan. She soaks up my breakfast and then scrapes the rotted remains of the possum from the washroom floor, maggots and all. She certainly is a brave woman. With the stench in the basement still so over-powering, we agree that what just happened is too gross to ever speak of again and finally head upstairs.

With my mouth freshly cleaned and hair redone, we make our way out. Brandon starts to say something but I glare at him. He obviously gets the message and immediately shuts his mouth while turning his eyes to the ground. The bag containing the disgusting remains is dropped at the curb and we all quietly pile into the vehicle. Still shaking, I wonder what else could possibly go wrong today.

Chapter 5

Crescent Falls High is much larger than I would have expected a small town school to be. A tall digital sign stands near the entrance to the busy parking lot, flashing the words Welcome Back Cougars. I imagine an older woman chasing after a young man and a small chuckle escapes my lips. I guess my new school mascot is a cougar.

We pull into a tree lined parking lot, which is already filled with vehicles surrounded by groups of lounging students. After confirming one more time that I'll be fine, my mother stops long enough for me to quickly hop out. She waves while turning back onto the street. As I pass by the other students on my way towards the school, I hear them whispering amongst themselves. Who is she? Is she new? Where did she get those clothes?

A narrow walkway leads from the parking lot to the main doors of the school. It is a red brick, two-story building complete with the name Crescent Falls High in big block letters above the entrance. In the middle of a rounded garden, surrounded by stone benches, a pole stands with our flag flying high. Going to enter I notice the same image of a large cougar, positioned as if ready to pounce, on both glass doors. They sure do display a lot of pride here.

Inside, the first thing that catches my eye is a large mural of another cougar with the words Cougars Care beneath it. Shaking my head and thinking that maybe they have went a little too far promoting their mascot, I head towards the main office.

"Good morning dearie. How can I help?" A short, husky receptionist, who is wearing way too much makeup, greets me at the front desk with a smile.

I give her my name and explain that I'm new and looking for my class. She tucks an unruly lock of gray hair behind her ear and starts typing away on a keyboard. When she finally finds my schedule, she prints it out and hands me a copy. Looks like my first class is science and somewhere on the second floor. The receptionist is trying to explain how to get there, when a thin young man enters the office.

"Hey, Judy. Here's the key." He says, passing the receptionist a silver key with a tag attached that reads AV Room.

"Adam, this is Lily Crawford." Judy says while placing the key in a drawer. "She just moved here. Do you mind showing her around?"

"Sure. I'd love to." He answers, looking me up and down through his thick glasses.

Adam holds the door for me as we leave the office. What a gentleman, I think to myself.

"Say hi to your father for me." Judy calls as the door slowly closes behind us.

Back in the main lobby, which is now crowded with students hurriedly moving in all directions, Adam asks to look at my schedule. A smile appears on his face while he briefly reads it over. Apparently we have a few classes together, including my first, which is totally fine with me.

We are crossing the lobby, towards a wide staircase leading up to the second floor, when I spot a muscular student with a buzz cut. The blue jacket he wears has a large cougar on the back. He is surrounded by a group of tall, skinny blonde girls which are basically hanging off of him. He certainly doesn't seem to mind. As we pass by, he sticks his large foot out. It all happens so quickly. Adam falls face first, his glasses slipping off and sliding across the floor. Buzz Cut calls him a loser while the girls giggle. Other students just point and laugh. I'm caught off guard and expecting an all-out brawl between the two of them. Amazingly though, Adam simply picks up his glasses, brushes himself off and keeps walking as if nothing happened.

"What was that all about?" I ask, following closely behind.

"That would be Jimmy. The *great* quarterback of the football team." He replies, sarcasm dominating his voice.

"Why didn't you do something about it?" I ask as we arrive on the second floor, which is just as crowded as the first. Making our way down the hall and around the clusters of students, he explains how it is a common occurrence for people to pick on him and treat him the way they do. Jimmy isn't the only one but he is the most public about it. Not wanting to start a fight or do anything that could cause problems for his father, Adam has learned to live with it.

I find myself feeling sorry for him but at the same time admiring his strength. If that were me, I would have knocked Jimmy's block off and probably been suspended on the spot.

Adam shows me to my brand new tiny locker and, changing the subject, asks how I like the town and school so far. I explain that I haven't seen much of the town yet and go on to describe the horrible event that happened this morning. He doesn't cringe at all. In fact he reminds me of my brother, thinking all that nasty, creepy stuff is cool.

I jump when the warning bell rings loudly overhead. Guess I'm still a little on edge after my earlier escapade. After shutting my empty locker, Adam leads me to class, weaving our way between the other students. Someone runs by me without slowing down, hitting me with their heavy backpack. Man these people are rude and pushy.

"So, who is your father anyway?" I inquire as another student rushes past me.

We turn a corner and stop outside an open classroom. Adam turns to me and motions towards the open door, grinning.

"You're about to find out."

Chapter 6

We enter the classroom to find most of the students standing in various groups, chatting quite noisily. There are four counters around the room, each with their own sinks and Bunsen burners, surrounding desks which are arranged in the center. A few preppy blonde girls, some of whom I recognize from earlier, are huddled off to the side, in their heels and short skirts. They start to whisper amongst themselves, keeping their eyes on us. Standing at the front of the room, we glare back in their direction.

"Don't worry about them. They're just your typical stuck up rich girls... and our school's *wonderful* cheerleaders. I like to call them the Snobettes." Adam says loud enough for them to hear. This guy seems to love his sarcasm.

They are practically foaming at the mouth and about to pounce when a girl carrying a satchel over her shoulder rushes up to us. I swear she could have been plucked from some rock band's music video. An ash gray beret covers short, black hair streaked pink here and there. Her dark eyeliner matches the black vest she wears over a white shirt. With a large smile, she playfully hits Adam's arm with her closed fist.

"Lily, this is Amy." Adam introduces us. "She's one of the good ones."

Amy readjusts the strap on her shoulder and sticks out her hand. We shake and she makes it a point to tell me that any friend of Adam's is a friend of hers. We find a few seats near the back of the room and I find out that Amy is the editor-in-chief of the school newspaper. Adam and Amy became good friends due to the occasional collaboration between the paper and the AV club, not to mention the constant harassment from others.

While we are getting to know each other, a young looking man whom I assume is our science teacher and Adam's father, enters the room. When I think science teacher, the first image that comes to mind is an old, nerdy type with crazy hair, glasses and a lab coat. This guy however is quite the opposite. He has light brown hair that is cut short and peppered with a little gray here and there. Deep, blue eyes that I could lose myself in for hours. A tight, black shirt covers his surprisingly muscular body, not doing a very good job of hiding anything. I feel like I could start drooling at any moment.

My fantasy comes crashing to a halt however, when he takes his place at the front of the room and slams his briefcase on the counter. Everyone jumps. Standing there with the periodic table displayed behind him, he bellows for everyone to find their seats.

"Hey Lily," Adam whispers while tapping my shoulder. "Don't let any more flies in." A barely audible laugh escapes his lips while I quickly cover mine with both hands.

Once everyone is settled, Adam's father turns and writes his name across the blackboard for all to see. Mr.

Walker is scrawled in large letters and underlined twice. Dropping the chalk back into its place, he then turns and addresses the class.

"My name is Mr. Walker and I will be your science teacher this year. Do as I say and everything will be fine but if you disobey me, there will be consequences." He says before picking up a clipboard. "Now let's take attendance."

After calling out names and having everyone nervously reply with "here", we go over first day stuff and then are told to form lab groups which we will be in for the rest of the semester. Of course Adam, Amy and I form our own group while the Snobettes form one as well. The rest of the class is pretty uneventful as Mr. Walker goes over the basics and explains what we should expect for the rest of the term. The bell rings and the three of us agree to meet up later for lunch.

Once my morning classes are finally over, my growling stomach and I find our way through the halls to the cafeteria. Adam and Amy are patiently waiting for me just outside the double doors and their eyes light up as they notice me heading towards them. The room is already packed with students and teachers both. There is an aisle, which leads to the busy food line, down the center of the room, with five rows of tables on either side. I notice Mr. Walker seated at one of the far tables with some of the other faculty members. Jimmy is here too, in one of the aisle seats, surrounded by all his cronies, including the Snobettes from science class.

The line continues to inch along. Eventually we reach the front where we get our share of Caesar salad, slimy mashed potatoes, what I can only assume is mystery meatloaf and a dish of chocolate pudding. At least the salad and pudding don't look too bad. We each grab a drink and begin the hunt for a free table. Adam is walking down the aisle ahead of me, talking over his shoulder, when a foot shoots out in front of him. I try to warn him but it's in vain. Adam falls face first into his chocolate pudding, causing it to splatter in all directions.

The room erupts in laughter while many of the students point and shout out "Loser!" Amy and I help Adam to his feet, pushing away the tray. There is chocolate pudding smeared all over his face and hanging from his glasses. Even his hair is streaked with chocolate. We all turn to see whose foot it was that caused the incident. Our suspicions are confirmed when we see Jimmy, with an evil grin, watching us while his friends laugh hysterically.

"I thought dessert was supposed to be saved for last." Jimmy says, trying to taunt Adam.

This causes everyone to laugh even louder. Adam's hands are balled into fists and he looks like he is about to explode on Jimmy, which I would totally support. Instead though, he spins on his heels and marches out of the cafeteria.

"Yeah, you walk away!" Jimmy calls after him. "Coward!"

"What the hell is your problem?" I slam my hands on the table in front of Jimmy as I lay into him. "Why can't you just leave him alone?"

"I guess he's even more of a wimp than I thought." Jimmy says, sneering at the both of us while his friends snicker. "Since he needs a couple girls to fight his battles for him."

I am about to deck him but Amy talks me down. We decide to go search for Adam instead. It ends up being fruitless however. We don't find him in the halls and there is no answer when we call into the boy's washrooms. We give up our hunt when the bell sounds, signaling the end of lunch. Making plans to meet out front after school, we go our separate ways.

After math, the worst subject of all, and a history class that almost put me to sleep, I am relieved and a little ecstatic when the last bell rings. As everyone begins packing up, my pocket begins to vibrate. Pulling out my phone I see a message from my mother. She is going to pick Brandon up and there might be a surprise waiting when I get home. Way to be cryptic Mom. Stopping at my locker, I drop off my books before heading out front to meet Amy. There is no sign of her. Where could she be?

I'm waiting by the main doors, admiring the cougars and maybe starting to like them a little, when I hear yelling coming from the parking lot. Rushing along the path, I turn the corner to see a group of students surrounding a severely vandalized car. Jimmy is on his knees inspecting one of the tires.

The boy closest to Jimmy shoves his phone in his pocket. "They're on their way, man." He says, placing his hand on Jimmy's shoulder. Nodding, Jimmy stands.

"Who did this?" Jimmy shouts, glaring at the crowd.

Nobody responds. Looking around I spot Amy next to one of the trees at the edge of the lot. I make my way over to find out what's going on. Apparently Jimmy came out after class to find all four of his tires slashed and his windshield smashed in. He must have really pissed someone off.

"Where's Adam?" I ask. "Have you seen him yet?"

Amy shrugs. "Not since lunch." She answers.

A tow truck appears, honking its horn to clear a path through all the gawking students. Multiple teachers have also arrived on the scene, including Mr. Walker. They try to keep the other students at a safe distance. Jimmy continues screaming while his car is moved onto the flatbed, ready to be taken away. He hops in the truck as Adam turns the corner and enters the parking lot. Jimmy spots him and shouts through the open window as they drive off, "You'll pay for this, Walker!"

Chapter 7

The three of us finally leave the school grounds. Adam and Amy have offered to show me around town, now that everything has settled down and most of the onlookers have moved on. They insist on pointing out the places to go and the places to avoid. What every new girl in town needs to know. I'm actually looking forward to our little tour and getting to know my way around my new home.

"So did you do it or not?" Amy questions Adam as we turn onto the sidewalk.

"Of course not!" Adam adamantly replies, looking hurt that she would actually think he was capable of doing that.

He had honestly seemed as surprised as everyone else when he first entered the parking lot and saw what was going on. Sure, he and Jimmy have their differences, but Adam doesn't seem like the type to destroy someone's property.

"Where did you go during lunch?" Amy continues her interrogation. "We tried searching for you."

Adam explains that after being humiliated in front of everyone, he hid in one of the stalls in the boy's washroom. He had heard us calling but had decided not to answer, instead standing on the seat to hide his feet in case we had gone in. He tells us how he spent the rest of his lunch cleaning pudding from his face and hair. I feel sorry for him and we spend the next few awkward minutes in silence.

They lead me further away from the school, winding back and forth through various tree lined streets. Our first stop is "The Park" as everyone calls it, even though the actual name on the wooden sign is MacLeod Park. Green grass as far as the eyes can see, spotted with numerous leafy trees for shade. There is an extravagant playground for children as well as a small water park with colorful overhead fountains. Young children are laughing happily and chasing each other through the playground while their parents keep a watchful eye from their benches in the shade. Another young boy is loudly crying at the top of a twisty, yellow slide, calling for his mother. Some older children are running under the tall fountains in the water park, playfully spraying each other with large, plastic water guns.

As we pass through the surprisingly enormous park, I see there is also a soccer field and a baseball diamond, both of which are currently in use. We make sure to keep our distance so as not to be hit with any stray balls. Watching them play brings back memories of New York and my old soccer team.

A large, unleashed St. Bernard surprises me as it leaps up, knocking me backwards to the ground. While I rest on the cool grass, the dog lets go of a soggy tennis ball and starts slobbering all over my face. Everyone gets a good laugh out of that.

"No!" A young guy, with short blonde hair, calls to the dog. "Max, come here." When the dog doesn't listen he pulls the large fur ball off of me. Amy, smirking, helps me to my feet.

"I'm so sorry. Max is just really friendly." He apologizes while holding the dog at bay. "My name's Luke."

"Lily." I reply, brushing myself off.

We spend the next few minutes talking. He is an artist, a year older than us and taking a year off before applying to college.

"Well Lily," Luke says, tossing the dripping tennis ball for Max. "Maybe I'll see you around." He flashes me a grin before running off after the dog. I am left blushing, embarrassed and speechless, while Amy snickers behind me.

Leaving the park, we continue the tour through town. They walk me past the cemetery where teenagers like to hang out after dark and drink, among other things. I'm told that the cops have had to chase kids away on numerous occasions. It is set back from the road and mostly hidden by the surrounding trees. I imagine it would be fairly creepy in the middle of the night. It certainly wouldn't be my first choice for a hangout.

We pass my brother's school, which now looks deserted, and head down Main Street. There are various family run shops selling anything anyone would want including clothing, electronics, toys, books, hardware and of course food of all kinds. Windows are filled with lovely displays, showcasing what each store has available. They point out the town hall with the flag high above. From

31

where I'm standing in the center of town, I can see Crescent Falls General Hospital in the distance.

Following the smell of cinnamon, we end up at a small corner café. The name Clara's is displayed elegantly above the door, next to an image of a steaming cup of coffee. Loving it so much, I stand there for a moment, breathing in the aroma. The café is a buzz with what appears to be mostly students.

"What can I get you guys?" A pleasant young woman behind a glass counter, filled with tempting cakes and pies, takes our order. She provides me with the most delicious latte I have ever tasted. We find a table out on the patio and enjoy our drinks in the sun.

"So, what do you think of Luke?" Amy asks coyly, nudging my arm with her elbow.

I try to reply calmly, while slowly sipping my latte, but only manage to stutter, "He s-s-seems... nice."

"So," Adam adjusts himself in his chair. "What was New York like?" He asks, trying to change the subject.

"Do you think he's hot?" Amy inquires, totally ignoring Adam. She leans forward with both hands around her cup.

Unsure of how to respond, I utter, "Ummm-"

"OK. Time to go." Adam stands, cutting me off before I can say anything too incriminating. Amy relents and after finishing the rest of our beverages, we leave. As we are walking down Main Street, Adam graciously offers to walk me home. Getting there on my own could be troublesome. When I think my tour is about to come to an end, Amy suddenly stops and exclaims excitedly, "Oh, let's show her the falls!"

Chapter 8

They both seem overly excited to show me the town's namesake. Adam appears to have received his second wind and totally forgotten about returning me home. I have to work to keep up as they lead me away from downtown. We arrive at the end of a deserted dead-end street. The last house I saw was at least a block away. A run down, chain link fence lies before us, engulfed by tall weeds and other shrubbery. A large yellow sign hangs crookedly on the fence, warning people to keep out. This area doesn't look like it has been maintained in years.

"Come on Lily." Adam and Amy call to me as they eagerly wade through the tall grass towards the fence.

Burrs stick to me as I push my way through weeds and swarms of tiny flies. Adam grabs a section of the fence and, lifting it away from the ground, holds it up for us. Amy, pressing her beret to her head and hugging her satchel close, ducks down low and passes under. I quickly follow in her footsteps, trying not to get my shirt caught on the fence. With us on the other side, Adam shows off by letting go of the fence, easily climbing to the top and leaping over.

"Thank you, thank you." He says, landing next to us and taking a bow.

Once he is finished with his grandstanding, Adam starts fighting his way through the overgrowth, following some unseen path. A bird darts out of the shrubbery to my left, startling me half to death, and flies off into the trees. As I stand there trying to catch my breath, I can hear Amy giggling ahead of me. Part of me wonders if they are just bringing me out here to see if the "Big City Girl" can handle it.

The path Adam has been following leads directly to the edge of the darkest woods I could ever imagine. The trees appear to go on forever with very little sunlight making its way through. I hear birds chirping high up in the tree tops.

"We have to go through there?" I ask, reluctant to enter the woods.

"It's just a few trees. The falls are on the other side." Adam quickly answers, dismissing my concerns, before charging off ahead.

At least the grass is not waist high in here, there is actually a visible path. I follow closely behind Amy as we hurriedly move along, trying to keep up with Adam.

"Get it off! Get it off!" Amy suddenly screams. She starts hysterically swiping at her face, dropping her satchel to the ground.

She has walked directly into a web. Who's the "Big City Girl" now, I think to myself. As Amy shrieks, terrified, a spider with a red body and black legs begins slowly crawling along the top of her beret, aiming for her forehead. It doesn't look like any spider I've ever seen. Without thinking, I quickly swat the beret from her head and watch as it sails into the brush along the side of the path. Adam, hearing the commotion, races to Amy's side. He tries calming her down while gently lifting the silky threads from her face.

"Why did you knock my hat flying?" Amy asks, turning to me with a look of confusion.

After a few moments of debating whether or not to tell her, I eventually say, "I didn't think you wanted a giant spider on your face too."

Amy's eyes go wide as she visibly shudders. Adam places a hand on her shoulder and removes the last thread from a strand of pink hair. After calming herself, Amy picks up her satchel and finding her beret, gives it a good shake.

"We are going to get to those falls." Amy says, returning the beret to its place on her head. "Even if it kills me." Adam and I follow as Amy, more determined than ever, takes the lead.

We exit the woods and I find myself in a stunning oasis. The famous Crescent Falls majestically cascades over a mountain face, crashing into a deep, blue pool below. I feel the cool mist on my skin as I approach. Sunlight shines through openings in the canopy of luscious leaves, causing the pool to sparkle. A trail snakes its way through the surrounding trees to the top of the falls. Large stones and roots jut out of the ground around the water, creating some perfect places to unwind.

We all remove our shoes and wade into the water. It is much deeper than I realized, but extremely refreshing. After a few minutes of laughing and playfully splashing each other, Amy and I retire to one of the large stones. Adam stays behind, chasing a school of minnows around the pool.

"This place is beautiful. Why was it fenced off?" I ask as we dangle our feet in the water. I lean back, letting the warm sun caress my face.

"Well... People used to come here all the time, but a few years ago there was... a horrible accident." Amy stares down into the blue water, a distant look on her face. "Kids used to jump from the top of the falls all the time. They weren't supposed to but they did it anyway." She pauses for a moment, then taking a deep breath, she turns to me and continues. "One day Mark, a boy from our school, decided to jump." She lifts her feet from the water and hugs her knees to her chest. "He hit his head on one of the rocks." Amy's eyes glisten in the sunlight as the tears begin to form. "He survived, but hasn't been the same since. They decided to fence off the area after that to keep people out and to prevent it from ever happening again."

"I'm so sorry, Amy." I finally manage to say. "Were you two close?"

"We worked on the paper together and saw each other almost every day." Amy replies, working hard to keep her composure as she wipes away a tear. "He was taken out of school, his family moved and no one has heard from them."

I hold her close for a couple minutes while trying to imagine what it must have been like for her. Deciding it is time to head home, we call Adam out of the water and make our way back through the woods. On the street, Amy parts ways with us. Adam still insists on walking me home. We arrive in front of my house as the sun is setting over the rooftops, turning the sky a lovely, pinkish red.

"We should do this again sometime." Adam says before leaving me on the porch and jogging down the road. Without having a chance to reply, I simply watch him fade into the distance while wondering what he meant.

After wiping my shoes on the welcome mat, I open the front door only to be immediately ambushed by a yellow lab. Suddenly my mother is there laughing and pulling my attacker back into the house.

"Lily," She says, calming the dog by scratching behind its ear. "Say hello to Zoey."

Chapter 9

"PICK AN R!" An elderly woman yells at the contestant on her television screen, pointing at it with her fork. She lets out an irritated sigh when the person chooses an L instead. The buzzer follows. It's the same routine every night. She sits on her white and pink floral sofa, eats dinner off a tray and watches her favorite game show, as frustrating as it can be. Two white Persians lay curled up behind her on the back of the sofa while a Siamese lies on the matching recliner. Her fourth and last cat, a calico, grooms itself on the sill of the open living room window. Moonlight shines down on the cat as the sound of crickets chirping flows in on the cool night breeze.

The show comes to an end as the young contestant guesses the wrong phrase, to the elderly woman's chagrin. She knew the answer the whole time. After finishing the rest of her microwave dinner, she stands and wheels the squeaky tray into the dimly lit kitchen. A filthy chandelier, with only one working bulb, hangs in the center of the room. The counter is piled high with food encrusted dishes and the garbage is filled to the point of overflowing. A cockroach scuttles away from the trash as she enters the room, disappearing into the darkness under the fridge.

"TIMOTHY!" She screams for her son in a hoarse, raspy voice.

Banging can be heard on the stairs leading up from the basement as if it were a pack of wild animals. A wooden door swings open into the kitchen and her thirty-four year old son appears. He is grossly overweight, and has a scruffy beard that hasn't seen a trimmer in weeks. A white t-shirt, stained with tomato sauce, clings to him, not quite covering the lower half of his stomach. Wearing a pair of ripped jean shorts that are way too short for him, let alone anyone else, he stands in the doorway with a look of annoyance. How dare she call him away from his computer.

"What do you want Mom?" He asks, with one hand scratching his beard and the other scratching where the sun don't shine.

"I told you if you were going to stay here that you had to pull your weight." She starts ranting. "The dishes need to be done, the garbage is overflowing and now we've even got friggin' roaches. Clean up after yourself! I'M NOT YOUR FREAKING MAID!"

He raises his hands as if to defend himself.

"OK... Alright... I'll take care of it." He replies with a sigh.

She retires back to the living room, leaving Timothy standing in the kitchen alone. Filling the sink with warm soapy water, he leaves the dishes to soak. Stuffing it as full as it will go before bursting, he ties off the garbage bag. Standing there with the plastic bag in hand, fluid dripping from the bottom, he notices another roach scurry under the fridge to join its companion. *I would hate to see what's under there*, he thinks to himself.

Save for the moonlight, and the stars in the sky, the night is quite dark. Timothy notices how different the temperature is outside and can't wait to get back to his cool basement and chat room. Sweat starts to soak through his white shirt, displaying folds he would rather keep hidden. As he waddles over to the dented can, resting against the house, the quiet sets in. The chirping that had been echoing across the surrounding fields is gone. The only things that can be heard are the television and the cat on the window sill above. The lack of noise becomes unsettling and Timothy quickly lifts the lid and tosses the bag in. The spider blending in with the home's red brick façade goes unnoticed. With a feeling of apprehension, Timothy rushes back inside as fast as his stubby little legs can carry him.

He begins scrubbing the soaking dishes, his anxiety subsiding. Upon hearing him enter, his mother joins him in the kitchen. Feeling guilty, she apologizes and, grabbing a towel, assists him with the dishes. Laughter and cheers fill the room as a comedy program plays on the television. A tiny black leg appears on the window sill next to an oblivious cat. The spider inches closer and closer until it brushes up against its furry tail. Startled, the cat lets out a meow which is muted by the television. Turning, it paws at the spider until it falls to the ground below.

Returning to its curled up position, the cat enjoys the night air unaware of another spider slowly descending on a silky web. Landing gently on the feline's head, it sinks its fangs in. The cat yelps while frantically pawing at its ear. As it does, another drops from above, then another, and another. They swarm from all directions, each one biting into the cat's flesh as it attacks. Eventually its whole body is covered in a rippling blanket of red and black. The cat, terrified, feels them crawling over every inch of its body, their tiny legs combing through its fur. In an attempt to escape, it leaps from the sill to the ground below. Running is futile. After a few feet, its legs become stiff. Unable to move, the cat tries to howl. Nothing comes out. Its whole body has become rigid. Paralyzed, it falls to its side, eyes wide open. Still able to see, the cat watches in horror as the swarm of spiders once again engulfs it.

In the middle of the driveway, the cat is slowly turned over and over as silky strands are wrapped around its furry body. It watches helplessly as the covering gradually gets closer and closer to its face. Then everything goes dark. With the last strand in place, the spiders disappear into the grass, dragging the doomed cat behind them.

With the dishes done, Timothy says goodnight to his mother and returns to his basement sanctuary. The elderly woman places a few small dishes on the counter before opening the fridge and removing a couple cans of cat food. The Siamese and both Persians race into the kitchen and rub against her legs. She laughs to herself. *They always know when it's dinner time.* Placing the full dishes on the floor she realizes the calico is nowhere in sight.

"Here Patches." She calls to him, clanging the tin against one of the small dishes. When he doesn't appear she checks the living room, finding only the open window. The sound of crickets chirping floats in through the open space. Brushing a random strand of silk out of the way, she sticks her head over the sill and calls into the night, "PATCHES!"

Chapter 10

The next morning a white and blue car, with the words Crescent Falls Police Department written on the side, screeches to a halt in front of the school. The door swings open as I approach. An officer with short brown hair, wearing a pair of dark sunglasses and a navy blue uniform, steps out. Passing the crowd of gawking students, he pulls open the main doors. With him gone, the group surrounds the car, peeping in the windows. Even I stop to take a quick look before entering the building.

As I figured, the lobby is packed with students, each trying to get a look at the cop. Standing by the doors, trying to avoid being trampled, I can make out Judy talking quietly with him next to the main office. She nods, her gray hair swishing back and forth, and then they both disappear inside. As the lobby gradually clears, I make a beeline for the stairs.

"Have you seen Adam? I can't find him anywhere." Amy appears beside me while I'm struggling with my locker. She watches while chewing on her lower lip.

"Damn thing!" I slam my fist against the locker door and it pops open. Not today locker, not today. "Why so worried?" I say, turning to Amy. "I'm sure he's fine.

We'll see him in class." Grabbing my books, I slam the metal door closed.

"Did you see the cop?" Amy asks, twirling strands of hair around her finger. "I know Adam said he didn't do it, but what if he did? What if they arrest him? What if-"

"Amy, calm down! He didn't do anything!" I interrupt, trying to keep her worrying to a minimum. "Let's just get to class. We can talk to him there... OK?"

When we arrive though, even I begin to worry. Neither Adam nor his father is there. The room gets quiet as everyone watches us enter. We almost make it to our seats before it starts.

"Adam's going down!" One of the Snobettes calls out. "He's gonna pay for destroying Jimmy's car!"

"He's getting what he deserves!" Someone else shouts. "He'll-"

"That's Enough!" A young woman enters, placing her purse on Mr. Walker's desk. She stares at all of us. We quietly take our seats.

"My name is Mrs. Davis." She introduces herself. "I'll be filling in for Mr. Walker while he's away. I would like our time together to be enjoyable," She says, looking around the room. "But talk like that will not be tolerated." Her eyes come to rest on one of the snickering Snobettes. Pointing towards the hallway, she says, "If anyone has a problem with that, there's the door." The snickering stops almost immediately. "Alright, now can someone tell me where Mr. Walker left off?"

We are beginning our assignment when the overhead system comes to life, calling one of the students down to the office. The student slowly rises and leaves the room, numerous oohs and aahs following. Amy and I return to the group assignment only to be interrupted again a few minutes later. The overhead calls another student away. This continues all morning until they eventually get to my name.

After nervously collecting my things, I leave the classroom, quickly making my way to the main office. As I enter, Judy ushers me towards a small conference room. A wooden rectangular table sits in the center of the room, not leaving space for much else. The officer from earlier is on one side of the table, various files scattered before him. Principal Harris is positioned across from him, nervously pulling at a loose thread on his sleeve. Judy deposits me in the room and then scurries away. Smiling my way, Principal Harris nods towards an ominous chair at the head of the table. I place my stuff next to the chair and take a seat. I can feel the officer's eyes burning into me as he watches my every move. Why do I feel like I'm on trial for murder?

"My name is Sam Wright and I'm the chief of police here in Crescent Falls," the officer introduces himself as a slight hint of a smile crosses his face. He checks a folder in front of him. "And you are?"

"My name's L-L-Lily Crawford," I manage to stammer. Principal Harris sits quietly next to me, now picking at his fingernails. He appears to be as anxious as me, obviously wanting this to be over.

"I believe you met my wife and son the other day. You just moved in next door to us didn't you?" Chief Wright asks in a surprisingly pleasant tone.

"Yeah, Mary and Devon, right? They came over when we were moving in." I reply. "They seem really nice. I think Devon's in the same class as my brother."

He nods, leaning back in his chair. I glance at the folder open in front of him and notice my name written across the top. Why does he have a folder with my name on it?

"So how are you enjoying the new school?" He asks, seeming genuinely interested. "I hear you're making some new friends."

"I've made a couple new friends." I answer. "Why?"

"I hear you've been spending time with an Adam Walker. Is that right?"

"Ye-"

"Does he get bullied a lot?" He cuts me off before I can finish. "Maybe by a student named Jimmy?"

"Yeah, Jimmy's a dumb jock who needs-"

"So," He cuts me off again, the pleasant tone gone. Leaning forward he clasps his hands in front of him. Getting real close, he says, "Is that why *you* destroyed his car?"

Chapter 11

"**I** didn't have anything to do with that!" I exclaim, shocked that I am suddenly being blamed. My palms start to sweat as I continue wringing my hands beneath the table. Principal Harris finally stops fidgeting and rises, seemingly about to intervene. Chief Wright only has to shake his head and Principal Harris begrudgingly returns to his seat. The Chief's accusing eyes remain focused on me.

"What makes you think I destroyed Jimmy's car?" I inquire, confused as to where all this is coming from. A bead of sweat begins to roll down my forehead. I quickly wipe it away with the back of my arm.

"Well Lily, where should we begin?" He asks, leaning back in his chair again. "Why don't we start back in New York?"

Damn! I knew this would come back to haunt me some day. The Chief continues to watch me as if waiting for a response, but I have no intention of making his job any easier. When I keep mum, he sighs and says, "It's my understanding that you were suspended last year for assaulting another student. I'm surprised they never pressed charges. The poor girl ended up in the hospital, didn't she?"

The "Poor Girl" was Jessica, the biggest bitch in school. She made a comment about my parent's divorce, saying that my dad was leaving because my mom was terrible in bed. I freaked, punched her multiple times in the nose and broke it in three places. I want to say she deserved everything she got, but only manage, "Yeah, but-"

"So obviously you have a problem controlling your temper." Chief Wright says, not waiting for me to finish. "On top of that I have multiple witnesses which confirm there was a confrontation in the cafeteria yesterday." He pulls a small notepad from his pocket. "I hear you were quite upset over what happened to Adam." Flipping open the notepad, he scans the first page. "Apparently you got in Jimmy's face before storming off and disappearing for the rest of lunch. This tells me you had motive and opportunity." He stares me dead in the eyes. "Maybe your temper got the better of you... again?"

"I didn't disappear. I was with Amy Vail all through lunch." I say. I'm not about to take the blame for this. "We were searching everywhere for Adam. He took off after what happened and we wanted to make sure he was OK. If you don't believe me, just ask Amy."

"Oh I will." He replies coldly, writing something in his notepad. "But in my experience, friends lie for friends."

That's the last straw. I'm sick of being accused of something I didn't do.

"Isn't there some rule or law about questioning students like this?" I ask, my voice rising. "Shouldn't I have my mother here... or a lawyer?"

"Why? We are only talking." He answers, closing the notepad and returning it to his pocket. "Do you think you need a lawyer?"

"OK, I'm done." I say, knocking the chair over as I stand. "My mother will be hearing all about this."

Chief Wright rises as well, probably in an attempt to stop me. Before he has a chance to say anything though, Principal Harris finally opens his mouth. "I think we are done here." He says, coming to my defense. "Lily, you can go." I grab my stuff and leave the room, slamming the door behind me.

The bell rings as I enter the lobby. I listen as classroom doors open and the clamor of students gets closer. Within moments, they are flocking past me. Blood still boiling, I cut through the crowd with no intention of returning to class. Reaching the main doors, I push my way through, letting them hit hard against the wall.

"Lily, wait up!" Turning, I watch through the glass as Amy bulldozes her way through the droves of students. "So, what did they want?" She asks, following me away from the school.

I detail the whole frustrating event for her, explaining how the police are trying to pin the destruction of Jimmy's car on me. She laughs when I tell her how I stormed out, leaving Principal Harris with his jaw on the floor.

"So what are *we* going to do for the rest of the day?" Amy asks, as we enter the parking lot.

I smile. Even though Amy and I have just met, I can tell we are going to be great friends. "Right now there is only one thing I want to do." I say, turning onto the sidewalk and leaving the school behind. "Let's go find Adam."

Chapter 12

"We're almost there," Amy says, leading the way. "His place is just down this street."

The homes in this area are enormous. I guess money is no issue for Adam. As we walk along the cement sidewalk, I notice how quiet it is. Everyone must be at work or school, everyone but us.

"Here it is." Amy brings us to a halt in front of one of the largest homes on the block. Wow! Approaching the front door of the three-story splendor, Amy and I step onto the covered porch. We are about to knock when the large wooden door swings open, startling us both.

"Oh, Amy, Lily," Mr. Walker stands before us, a disapproving look on his face. "Shouldn't you two be in school?"

I explain my morning to him as he leans against the door frame with his arms crossed, listening intently.

"I guess I can't blame you." He says. "I probably wouldn't want to stick around after that either. Besides, I did keep Adam home from school too." He passes us, leaving the door open, and starts down the steps. "If you're looking for Adam, he is up in his room." He continues down the driveway. "I have to go out for a while.

Be back soon." Hopping in his car, he backs out and drives off.

Amy leads the way inside and I shut the door behind us. I see a kitchen off to the right and to the left a large flat screen television hangs on the wall of what must be the living room.

"What are you doing here?" Adam appears on the stairs before us.

"We could ask you the same thing." I jokingly reply. "You missed all the fun." I continue as we follow Adam into the spotless kitchen, where even the counters and floors shine. He grabs a few bottles of water before leading us into the living room. Just like the kitchen, this room is immaculate. A fireplace complete with a mantle is the focus of the room. Numerous photos cover it, many of them depicting Adam with a beautiful woman.

"Is this your mother?" I ask, admiring the photos. "She's beautiful."

As I move along the line of photos, I get a glimpse of his mother's past. Laughing at the beach with Adam, holding his toddler sized hands in the park and even carrying him as a baby, swaddled in a blue blanket. At the end of the line sits a photo of her in a fabulous wedding dress, trying to cover her baby bump. Squinting, I realize the man in the tux next to her is Adam's father. He looks nothing like he does today and on passing glance you wouldn't even recognize him. The muscles are gone. It appears a strong wind could have snapped him like a twig. He raises a glass to someone out of frame. A toothpick swims in the red liquid while the attached Brazilian flag hangs over the rim.

"Her dress hides the pregnancy well." I state absentmindedly.

"What do you mean?" Adam asks.

"You can see creases here and here." With my finger, I circle the edges of the dress covering his mother's midsection. "It looks slightly rounded in front too. She's obviously pregnant." Adam steps forward, examining the photo. "But she's still beautiful." I add.

"She was," Adam hesitates. "She died a few years ago."

"I'm so sorry." I step back and take a seat next to Amy on the couch.

"It was a hit and run." Adam says, staring blankly at the line of photos. "They never did find the person." Opening his water bottle, he takes a drink. "My dad totally changed afterwards." He lowers himself into the armchair. "We hardly talk anymore, he works out all the time, and he has become really strict at school. He used to be the teacher everyone loved. Now they hate him and take it out on me." He turns to us with a fake smile. "But enough about that. What happened at school?"

I inform him of my morning in the makeshift interrogation room.

"How could they think it was me?" I ask, more to myself than anyone else.

"That may actually be my fault." Adam says with his eyes cast to the floor.

"WHAT?" I scream, leaping from the couch. Amy jumps up, standing between us. "What do you mean it's your fault?" I demand over Amy's shoulder.

"When I got home last night, the police were waiting for me." Adam says, unmoving from his place on the armchair, his eyes still focused on the floor. "Dad and Chief Wright were sitting around the kitchen table drinking coffee when I came in. He asked me all sorts of questions about Jimmy. Does he pick on me? Wouldn't I like to get back at him? He then went on to ask if I'd met anyone new or had any recent troubles with Jimmy." He raises his head. My anger fades as he looks at me though his glasses with red, watery eyes. "That's when I told him all about you. I told him how we had just met and that you were there when Jimmy tripped me in the lobby and during the fiasco in the cafeteria. It all just spilled out of me. I'm sorry."

"No, I'm sorry." I reply, returning to the sofa. "I wouldn't want you to lie to the cops. It would only make things worse. Besides, none of us did it anyway, so we have nothing to hide."

Both Adam and Amy nod in agreement. We drink in silence for a few minutes before I decide to try and lighten the mood.

"So, what's everyone doing this weekend?" I ask, receiving only questioning looks. "I'm celebrating my birthday with a pool party. There's going to be lots of music and cake." I watch as their eyes light up. "Who wants to come?"

They look at each other for a moment before they both shout simultaneously, "I do!"

Chapter 13

After spending another hour with Adam and Amy, I head home, intent on filling my mother in on today's events. Chief Wright shouldn't be allowed to do what he did. Unfortunately, when I arrive the driveway is empty. She must still be at work. As I approach the front door, barking erupts from inside. Our unthreatening guard dog Zoey appears in the window to my right, tail wagging furiously. I barely get the door closed before she clobbers me.

Brandon and I always wanted a dog, but living in an apartment in the big city, with parents that were always busy, it just wasn't feasible. However, now that we are in a home with a large yard, my mother didn't waste any time stopping by the local kennel and picking Zoey up. I think she wanted a dog just as much as we did, if not more.

"Well Zoey," I say, trying to avoid her tongue. "Since it's just you and me, what do you say we go for a walk?"

Her ears visibly perk up at the word walk. She starts racing back and forth as I repeat it a few times. OK, calm down silly dog. Grabbing her leash, I hook her up.

She walks me across the driveway and along the road. A couple tugs on the leash, followed by the word heel, finally gets things under control. Now leading, I steer us towards the park.

Except for a pair of young children and their watchful mothers, the playground is deserted. The waterpark is empty. No water is flowing. Zoey, being as friendly as she is, pulls on her leash. She attempts to race towards the kids but I hold her back, waving to the women as we pass.

Tennis balls fly as multiple games of fetch take place in the field beyond. One of the dogs notices me and comes bounding over, owner close behind.

"Hi Max." I say as he comes up short. Totally forgetting about me, he tries to *introduce* himself to Zoey.

"Max, come!" I watch as he actually turns and trots to Luke's side. Why wasn't it that easy yesterday? Reaching down, Luke scratches behind his ear. "That's my boy." He says before meeting me at the edge of the field. "And who is this beauty?"

"This is Zoey." I reply. "The newest member of the family."

"Well, hello Zoey." Luke says, kneeling in front of her. He sticks out his hand, but she goes straight for the face, her tongue washing his left cheek. "So, why aren't you in school?" He asks while Zoey's licking continues. "Cutting class already?" He adds jokingly.

"If only..." I answer, trailing off. Shaking my head, I lead Zoey towards a bench within the shade of a large tree. I remove the leash and watch her bound off towards Max. They appear to be having a grand time as she chases him and then he chases her. Looks like Zoey found a new best friend. Luke joins me on the bench, where I quickly recap my horrible morning.

"Wow..." Luke says while watching the dogs sniff at something on the ground. "I can't believe they are trying to pin the whole thing on you. I wonder why Chief Wright is being such a hard ass."

"Your guess is as good as mine." I reply. "It kind of feels like they just want to blame the new girl in town though." Glancing over at the dogs, I shout, "Hey, stop that!" It looks like Max got stuck playing leap frog. They both freeze and stare in our direction before racing over.

"What are you doing this Saturday?" I ask as Max leaps up, tongue hanging to the side.

"Nothing big planned yet." Luke replies, trying not to laugh as Max smothers my face with his slobbering tongue. "Why?"

My pulse suddenly starts racing. "You have to come to my birthday." I say. "It's kind of a pool party with music, lots of food... and cake. It'll be fun!"

"Sounds great." He catches me off guard with a wink. "I wouldn't miss it."

"That's g-great." I nervously stutter, reattaching Zoey's leash. I somehow manage to give him the time and place before leaving him alone on the park bench, Max by his side.

As we turn onto our street, my breathing begins to return to normal and I start to feel foolish for running off. There's no turning back now though, I guess. My mother is climbing out of her car when we start up the driveway.

"Hey Mom," I call, as Zoey drags me over to her. "Guess what happened today."

Chapter 14

The parking lot is nearly empty when Chief Wright pulls in. He rolls the cruiser into a spot close to the single-story, gray-brick building. Turning off the engine, he climbs out. The blue neon from the words Crescent Falls Police Department lights his way towards the entrance. Walking at a snail's pace, he stumbles on the uneven pathway that was supposed to have been fixed ages ago. Steadying himself, Chief Wright enters, looking forward to heading home to both his family and dinner.

Two large police badges, circled by the phrase To Serve And Protect, adorn the walls of the bland lobby. Four plastic chairs, two against each wall, sit empty; tall plants, plastic as well, act as dividers. A rounded wooden desk sits at the opposite end of the lobby, a sign shouting RECEPTION hanging above it. There is no bulletproof glass or security door to pass through. Behind the desk, a busty young woman files her nails, her shirt leaving nothing to the imagination. A cell phone vibrates on the counter next to her.

"Hi Chief," She says, replacing the nail file with her phone. "Did you, like, catch the bad guy?" Her red nails fly over the keys as she texts.

"Not yet Stacy," He replies with a disapproving shake of his head. "But I'm getting close." She doesn't even look up, instead focusing her attention on the device before her. With a sigh, Chief Wright continues to his office.

With the door shut behind him, Chief Wright finally allows himself to relax. Passing a wooden coat rack by the door, he takes a seat in the plush, leather swivel chair behind his large mahogany desk. To help release a little stress, he spins a couple times. The tension fades as the room circles him. When the dizziness starts to take hold, he stops, his eyes landing on a photo of what he treasures most in life. His family. Mary and Devon watch him from within their steel frame. Anxious to get home, he grabs a couple forms from a filing cabinet and grips the closest pen. As pen is about to touch paper, there is a knock at the door.

"Come in." He calls to the person standing on the other side. Officer Randall pops his head in, surveying the room. "Have a seat rookie."

"So Chief, how'd it go at the school today?" Officer Randall plops himself down in one of two matching leather chairs. "Did you find out what happened?"

"Well, the Crawford girl looks pretty guilty." He replies, beginning the paperwork before him. "I was questioning her when she stormed out. After that I talked to some other students but got basically the same story. Jimmy was picking on Adam Walker, the Crawford girl blew her top, threatened Jimmy and then disappeared. What she was doing during that time, no one knows."

"Man," Officer Randall plucks at his goatee. "It would be so much easier if the school just had a camera on the parking lot."

"Chief, I've got a Kate Stewart on line one for you... She, like, sounds pretty mad." Stacy calls from the lobby. *Geez, a little discretion would be nice,* the Chief thinks to himself.

"OK... I'll take it in my office." He sighs, knowing exactly what the call is about. Officer Randall slinks out of the room, giving the Chief his privacy. Picking up the receiver, he says, "This is Chief Wright. How can I help you?"

"This is Lily Crawford's mother. I understand you questioned and accused her of vandalizing another student's car today."

"We were talking today, yes." He responds, transferring the receiver to his other ear. "Just like I talked to most of the students at the school today."

"Well, I'm calling to tell you that if you ever talk to my daughter again, without me or a lawyer present, I will be suing you and your department. DO YOU UNDERSTAND?"

"Ye-"

The line goes dead before he can finish. Slamming the receiver back into place, he refocuses all his attention on completing the remaining paperwork, determined to make it home. With the final *i* dotted and *t* crossed, Chief Wright leaves and locks his office.

"Can you file these for me?" He asks, handing the forms to Stacy as he passes the reception desk.

"Sure, like, no problem Chief." Stacy replies, giving him a smile and a batting of her eyelashes.

Ignoring her obvious and frequent flirtations, he crosses the lobby, straightening the angled chairs in his path. "Have a good night everyone." He calls, backing towards the main entrance. Turning to push his way through the glass doors, he nearly collides with a younger, rounded fellow. The man nods at the Chief as he enters, waddling towards the reception desk. Wanting to forget this day ever happened, Chief Wright leaves, walking out into the night.

"Hi there cutie," Stacy says in her bubbly voice, watching the man approach. "How can I help you?"

"I'm here to report a missing cat. It went missing yesterday." He answers, his eyes drawn south of hers. "My mother looked everywhere but can't find him. Probably just took off, but she insisted I come in."

"I'm up here, cutie." She waves at him and then points to her face. His becomes beet red as he looks her in the eyes with his mouth agape. Giggling, Stacy hands the man a clipboard with an attached form; a pen dangles from the connected piece of string. "Don't leave out any details."

He sits in the seat furthest away, using the dividing plant to hide his embarrassment. The sweat from his palm coats the pen as he fills in every last space, trying to leave as much as possible. Name, color, size, and the list goes on. After adding his contact information, he hands the clipboard back to Stacy, dangling pen and all.

"Thanks Hun, we'll do our best to find..." She pauses to look over the form. "...Patches. And Timothy, if we have, like, any updates I'll give you a call." She says, batting her eyelashes once again.

Still red and unable to form a coherent sentence, Timothy nods and quickly waddles out the door. With the lobby again empty, Stacy takes the completed form, walks towards the rear of the station and enters the conference room. Officer Randall is working at a long, wooden table, paper piled around him. He watches with a worried expression as Stacy places the report on the largest stack. Turning to him she says, "We've got another one."

Chapter 15

Adam awakes to the birds singing and the sun shining through the white, plastic blinds covering his bedroom window. *Another wonderful day in the neighborhood*, he thinks to himself, dreading all the stares and hateful comments he is bound to receive at school. According to the digital display, it is just after six o'clock. Feeling refreshed and well rested, he pulls back his comforter and rolls out of bed.

His bare feet glide across the soft carpet as he makes his bed, ensuring everything is properly aligned and all the folds are smoothed out. *Nobody likes a messy bed*. As he turns to leave, urgently in need of the washroom, his eyes fall upon the photo resting on his nightstand. His mother stands before the falls, back when it was a large attraction, holding him in her arms. Her bright smile fills the frame.

As Adam stares into the picture, he remembers the good times they used to have. With his father constantly busy, they did everything together. Shopping, weekend lunches, and even taking in the occasional movie. She often referred to him as her best friend; he felt the same. All of that was taken away three years ago.

Weeks after the accident, Adam finally heard the whole story. It was Labor Day weekend and teens had once again flocked to Crescent Falls to party, among other things. Adam's father had some free time, so when Saturday evening rolled around, his parents decided it was date night. A fancy dinner at a gorgeous, high class restaurant in the city and then off to the theater. Adam, being mature for his age was allowed to stay home alone. He told them to have a great night and kissed his mother goodbye, for the last time.

Dinner was delicious and the classical music playing in the background added to the romantic atmosphere. They couldn't have asked for anything more. The theater was packed when they arrived, but they found a few empty seats in the back row. While everyone watched the movie, they instead were captivated by each other, making out like a couple of teenagers.

After the movie, they decided to head home. It was around midnight when they returned to Crescent Falls. Adam's mother insisted on picking up ingredients for her famous chocolate chip pancakes. Sunday's morning ritual. They stopped in front of the only twenty-four hour convenience store. When leaving, Adam's father realized he had forgotten his wallet inside. After telling Adam's mother to head to the car, he returned to retrieve it. Before the door could slide closed behind him, he heard the scream and squealing tires. The driver disappeared and his mother was pronounced dead on the scene. It wasn't until his father arrived home, alone, that Adam knew he would never see her again.

Unable to bear it any longer, Adam slowly opens his door and tip toes across the wooden floor towards the washroom. Afterwards, trying not to wake his father, he glides across the floor and down the stairs.

In the kitchen, he starts the morning routine of making breakfast and coffee for both of them. Grabbing a couple eggs from the fridge, he cracks them into the pan waiting on the stove. *Scrambled eggs sound good this morning.* Finding some bacon, he fries it up before using a travel mug to make his father's morning coffee. When he hears movement overhead, he calls out, "Dad, breakfast is ready!"

The scent of bacon and coffee fills the room as Adam sets the table, just right. His father arrives minutes later, clean shaven and dressed for work. A smile appears on his face as he breathes in the aroma. He takes a seat at the table while Adam serves.

"You know... you make breakfast for me every morning, make my coffee, clean... and I don't think I've ever thanked you." His dad says, in between sips of coffee. "I'm sorry for that... Your mom would be so proud... I am too."

"Don't worry about it." Adam replies, joining him at the table.

"No, it's important that I start to take notice of things. I've allowed myself to become isolated from everything and everyone I love, but no longer." He states before lightheartedly pointing his finger in the air. "You're going to see a change, starting today!"

All Adam can do is smile as he watches his father scarf down his food. He can't help but be reminded of how his mother used to make breakfasts like this. Laughing to himself, Adam wonders if this is how he looked when he wolfed it all down.

"And as far as this incident with the car." His father says in between bites. "I know you didn't do it, so don't worry about anything. I'll take care of it."

"Thanks Dad." Adam says, relieved. Knowing that his father believes in him means everything.

They spend the rest of breakfast discussing school and plans for after graduation. It is the first real conversation in a long time. Afterwards, Adam quickly cleans up and prepares for class. As they are about to run out the door, Adam grabs his father's forgotten travel mug from the counter. "Don't forget your coffee."

Chapter 16

I arrive at school in time to catch Adam and his father stepping out of their vehicle.

"Hey, Adam!" I shout, rushing towards them.

They both turn, waving in my direction as Mr. Walker leans over and whispers something in Adam's ear.

"I'll leave you two alone." Mr. Walker says with a smirk when I reach the vehicle. "See you in class."

With briefcase in one hand and a travel mug in the other, he strolls towards the school, not once looking back.

"So what was that all about?" I ask, adding, "What did he whisper to you?"

Adam's face turns bright red and he seems unsure of how to reply. I continue to stand there giving him the eye.

"He s...said...yo...you're..." He pauses, obviously having a hard time spitting it out.

"Well?" I say, hands on my hips. "Was it really that bad?"

"He said you're cute, OK!" He blurts out. I didn't think it was possible, but his face becomes an even dark-er shade of red. I can't help myself and suddenly erupt in laughter.

"I think my dad thinks there is something going on, but I made sure to tell him we are just friends." He hangs his head and stares at the ground, acting as if it all means nothing. "Can we just go in now?"

Getting myself under control, I nod and begin walking across the parking lot. Adam however, doesn't budge an inch. As he continues standing next to the vehicle, watching a crowd of students by the entrance, it becomes clear. He is worried about how they are going to treat him.

It strikes me that after yesterday I will probably be the next pariah. Making my way back to Adam's side, we stand frozen. As the minutes pass, an idea starts to form.

"Since your father already thinks we are together," I say. "Why not act the part? It will give everyone something else to talk about instead of the whole car thing."

"I don't know..." Adam replies, eyes still fixed on the crowd.

"All we would have to do is hold hands." I continue. "And maybe let people witness a couple quick kisses here and there. It'll be fun."

"But, what if-"

"Plus, since we will be spending most of our time together," I add as the thoughts keep coming. "We will have each other's back if anyone tries anything. What do you think?" I watch Adam, waiting for his reply.

"Screw them." He finally says. "Let's do it."

Smiling, I hold my hand out to him. "Alright, let's get started."

With his sweaty palm on mine, we make the trek towards what will surely be a barrage of questions and rude comments. Adam's hand tightens around mine as we approach the students near the entrance. I wince through the pain.

Someone notices us and shouts, "Look, here come the partners in crime!"

Everyone turns, looking in our direction. I feel their eyes on me, judging me.

"More like lovers in crime!" Another person yells, pointing at our hands.

The comments continue as a ring of students forms around us, expecting some sort of reaction. Well, I guess I should give the people what they want. Turning to face Adam, I take a deep breath and meet his lips with mine; Adam remains frozen in place. I can feel the warmth as his face begins to heat up.

Laughter gives way to cheering and even some hooting and hollering. Everybody seems to be enjoying our little show. Adam continues to stand stunned next to me as I break my lip lock with him. A few jokes are passed around at our expense. I'd much rather listen to comments about our romance than be involved in vicious rumors.

Principal Harris appears at the edge of the crowd, trying to settle everyone down. It's a struggle, but he gets the sound level to drop from a loud roar to a gentle simmer. After ushering people off, he steps closer, checking to see if we are all right. Adam manages to nod, still shocked I think. Feeling much calmer now, I have no problem filling him in on the situation, minus the part that it was fake of course. He flashes an approving smile as the warning bell rings.

We walk into class, still hand in hand. The Snobettes stand as we enter. When their mouths open I steel myself for the usual rude comments, but they come up short. Instead they, along with everyone else in class, start whispering amongst themselves while pointing in our direction. Haven't they ever seen two people in love, I laugh to myself. I notice Amy sitting at the back, her jaw reaching for the floor. Wait till she finds out the truth.

Mr. Walker startles us both when, from behind, he asks that we take our seats. We do, sitting next to an astounded Amy. Before she can begin her stream of questions, I lean over and quickly whisper, "I'll tell you all about it later."

Her mouth slowly closes; she seems content with that, for now. I turn to face the front of the room again, in time to see Mr. Walker wink in Adam's direction.

The morning seems to fly by; before I know it, the lunch bell is ringing. Meeting at my locker, we all walk together towards the cafeteria. On the way we fill Amy in. She doesn't seem to like the idea, but she says she'll help any way she can. I could swear her eyes flashed a dark shade of green.

I hadn't seen Jimmy all morning and was hoping that trend would continue; my luck disappears however, when we enter the cafeteria. He sits at a table along the far wall with a group of his cronies. Noticing us, he immediately stands. Adam goes rigid next to me, his grip once again tightening, threatening to crush my hand.

"So, I hear you're a couple now." Jimmy says as he approaches.

"Do you have a problem with that?" I reply, spitting out the words.

"Not at all... You losers deserve each other!" He comes to a stop in front of us, his eyes filled with rage.

Adam is suddenly moving, and fast I might add. He takes a shot at Jimmy, but misses unfortunately. His fist breezes by Jimmy's face as he dodges the punch, causing Adam to stumble forward. Silence settles over the cafeteria as everyone watches, waiting to see what will happen next. Adam catches himself and starts to turn back in Jimmy's direction. With all his strength, Jimmy throws a punch. He obviously expects to collide with Adam, finishing this one sided fight. It doesn't connect though. His fist stops inches from Adam's left eye; Jimmy, shocked expression and all, is dragged backwards.

"I wouldn't do that if I were you."

Chapter 17

"**D**id you hear me?" Mr. Walker grips the collar of Jimmy's shirt in his fist and roughly pulls him back. Principal Harris stands next to him. Amongst all the excitement, they had entered the cafeteria unnoticed. Jimmy struggles against the restraint but Mr. Walker is much larger and stronger. Eventually he relents and is walked out of the cafeteria, leaving the others behind.

In the hall, Mr. Walker releases Jimmy. Smoothing out his shirt, Jimmy turns and stares daggers at his captors. The rage inside him continues to grow. If he was any hotter, steam might start flowing from his ears.

"What were you thinking?" Mr. Walker inquires, already knowing the answer.

"That jerk deserves it!" Jimmy replies, overlooking the fact that the jerk is his interrogator's son. "He destroys my car and just walks away?"

"There is no proof he had anything to do with that." Mr. Walker counters, reflexively swatting the back of Jimmy's head.

"Regardless..." Principal Harris quickly interrupts their exchange before things get too out of hand. "Since nobody got hurt, we will drop it this time." He says, shooting Mr. Walker a disapproving look. Then, turning back to Jimmy, he adds, "If it happens again though you will be suspended, maybe even expelled, and definitely removed from football for the remainder of the year. Understand?"

"FINE!" Jimmy storms over to the nearest locker and slams his fist against it, leaving a large dent. Without looking back he strides down the hall in a huff.

Principal Harris, standing alone with Mr. Walker, wonders what to do with him. He is a wonderful teacher, or at least he used to be. Lately though, things have changed. Principal Harris decides he has to say something, especially after what he just witnessed.

"You can't go around grabbing and hitting students like that." Fearing confrontation, he then adds with a smile, "Even if they do deserve it."

Unable to see anything humorous about what just happened or the ramifications of his actions, Mr. Walker replies with, "Nobody hurts my son... Nobody."

Realizing there is no getting through to him, not now anyway, Principal Harris simply walks away, disappointed with both parties. When he disappears around the corner, the bell rings and the cafeteria starts to clear out. As the students pass by Mr. Walker, he receives multiple glares and even some frightened looks. A few of the other faculty members start to approach him. He quickly turns and heads in the opposite direction, ignoring their calls.

Mr. Walker's afternoon classes are nothing but awkward. Trying to teach a group of students who either hate you or are afraid of you isn't easy. *How did I ever let things get this bad?* The weather seems to be mimicking his mood, gradually turning miserable. The rain beats against the classroom windows, almost drowning out the whispers of his students.

Jimmy, the current bane of his existence, arrives for last class. He takes his seat with a smug look on his face. *How I wish I could just walk over there and knock it off*, Mr. Walker thinks to himself. *It's not like he wouldn't deserve it. Treating my son like dirt for no reason at all and getting away with it just because he is the quarterback of the football team. How is that right?*

Not a word is said between them though. Jimmy sits quietly, listening to the lecture as if nothing happened; Mr. Walker manages to get through without interruption. As class is coming to an end, a sudden flash of lightening followed by a loud, shaking thunder causes a few students to shriek. The others laugh.

"Well, on that note," Mr. Walker says, "I think we'll call it a day."

Books are slammed shut and bags are zipped. They all file out of the room, including Jimmy, still carrying his smug grin. Mr. Walker spends the next few minutes alone in the empty classroom with his thoughts. When the noise in the hallway begins to fade, he packs up and leaves, locking the door behind him.

Judy is hunched over the front desk, furiously writing away, when Mr. Walker enters the main office. Trying not to disturb her, he turns his attention to the wall of faculty mailboxes. Finding the slot with his name on it, all he sees is a booklet describing the new benefits package. As he slides it out of the box, a white envelope floats to the floor. Retrieving it, he turns the envelope over in his hand. It is completely blank.

"Judy, did you see who left this?" He asks, holding up the white envelope for her to see. She looks up briefly from her paperwork, taking a quick glance at the envelope in question.

"Nope, sorry Hun." She replies, returning her eyes to the documents in front of her.

Allowing his curiosity to get the better of him, Mr. Walker decides to see what's inside. *Maybe it will say who it's from,* he thinks to himself. Tearing open the sealed flap, he pulls out a blank index card. Flipping it over, he reads the three words written in thick, black marker.

I SAW YOU

Chapter 18

The rain falls in sheets as Jason and Beverly Cromwell pull into the driveway of their single-story bungalow. It has been a rough couple of days. Being in labor for thirteen hours was horrific for Beverly. Plenty of pain, dulled only by the requested epidural. She even screamed, multiple times, for the doctors to "Just rip this thing out of me!" The end result though was a beautiful, healthy baby boy whom they both couldn't love more.

The previous nine months had been wonderful. Jason waited on her hand and foot, even providing whatever strange mixture of foods she craved. They had been trying for close to a year to get pregnant and just when they were starting to lose hope, a plus sign appeared on the stick. They were ecstatic, rushing to tell their family, friends and any strangers that would listen.

Jason shuts off the engine and makes a mad dash for the front door, working to unlock it as he is pelted. With his hair soaked through and the water streaming into his eyes, blurring his vision, finding the lock becomes a difficult task. After a couple minutes, the key turns and the door swings open. Jason, now drenched, signals to his wife. She wraps her newborn son in the blue, crocheted blanket that her best friend made and gave to her during her baby shower. *I'm really going to have to learn this crochet thing*, she thinks to herself as her fingers slide over the soft wool.

When Jason sees Beverly give him the thumbs up through the streaks of rain covering the passenger side window, he lowers his head and sprints towards the car. He holds the door open for his wife as she climbs out and then, after slamming it shut behind her, they both race for the open front door of the bungalow.

Once inside, Jason grabs a couple large towels from the nearby closet. He drapes one over his head while handing the other to his wife. Uncovering her son, Beverly ensures he is completely dry before approaching the growing stockpile of colorful, baby blankets. *Apparently everyone and their mother thinks we need these*, she says to herself as she bundles him up.

"What do you want for dinner?" Jason asks, ruffling his hair with the towel as he enters the kitchen. "I think there are some burgers in the freezer."

"Anything would be good right now." Beverly replies, settling into her place on the living room sofa, her son in her arms. "I feel like I could sleep for a year."

With her feet up, Beverly begins to feed her son while a show about fairytale characters with memory loss plays out on the television. She is deeply engaged in the program when the strong scent of cooked meat causes her mouth to water.

"How much longer Jay?" Beverly calls.

"About five minutes." He replies, over the sound of spattering grease.

Deciding it would be best to put her son to bed, at least during dinner, Beverly forces herself to leave the comfy couch.

Light blue paint coats the walls of the small, yet cozy nursery. Multiple packages of diapers are piled near the door; a padded, wooden rocking chair is positioned in a corner. The window along the back wall sits slightly ajar, opposite a short dresser and a crib of the rocking variety. Beverly places her beautiful boy in the crib and kisses his forehead. She then returns to the living room, leaving the door open a crack.

As soon as Jason and Beverly sit down to eat, the crying starts. Beverly is on her feet in an instant, ready to race to her son's side, but Jason stops her.

"Let him cry it out." He says, coaxing her back to her place on the sofa. "I don't want us to become the kind of parents that coddle him every time he cries." He then adds with a smile, "We can check on him after dinner."

Staying put is a struggle for Beverly, but the crying fades and eventually stops. They finish eating as the television program comes to a close. Jason clears away the dishes and then they both quietly tip toe towards the nursery. Peering through the slightly open doorway, they notice the crib gently rocking back and forth in the dimly lit room. They give each other confused looks while wondering how that is possible.

Curious, they enter the room and flip on the light. Jason places his arm around his wife as they both step closer to the crib. Standing at the edge, they look in. Beverly lets forth a blood curdling scream. Hundreds of black and red spiders fill the crib from end to end. Their unmoving son is slowly being turned over and over as he is gradually covered in a silky web. Jason frantically swings, unsuccessfully, at the vicious spiders. As he swats some away, more appear to take their place. Beverly, still screaming and helpless, begins to feel lightheaded and lowers herself to the cold hardwood floor.

"I'll call 911." Jason says, unsure of what else to do.

As he rushes through the open door and enters the living room, he feels a sharp pain on the back of his head. The room starts to spin and he falls, barely catching himself with his outstretched hands. Jason rolls onto his back and looks up to see a dark, blurry figure standing over him. Then everything goes black.

Chapter 19

Jason awakes, feeling like he was hit by a train. The back of his head throbs with a pain that radiates throughout the rest of his body. When he reaches up to feel for a bump, Jason realizes he is unable to move his hands. *What's going on?* After blinking multiple times, he looks around the room. It is dark but he can just make out the chair in the corner, rocking. When he eventually sees the crib, it all starts to come back. The spiders covering his son, his wife screaming, and the dark figure looming over him.

His mind begins to race. *Where is my son? Is he alive? Where is Beverly? Who hit me?* He feels a cool sensation on the back of his legs and concludes that he is on the floor, propped up against the wall. Trying to stand, he finds that he is unable to move his legs either. He starts to struggle, a sense of urgency taking hold. As his mind begins to clear, he starts to notice the scraping of the rope against his skin. His clothing clings to him as he tries to twist free; he is soaked from head to foot.

When something brushes past his leg, he tries to scream. It is muffled by the gag in his mouth. *I have to get out of here. I have to get help.* Jason starts to scoot his way across the floor. *Move feet forward and pull. Again. And again.* Reaching the closed door, he turns over onto his knees and raises his bound hands. Grabbing ahold of the door knob, he turns and pushes. The door doesn't budge. He tries again but it is no use. He bangs on the door with his bound fists, making muffled cries for help; there is no answer.

Using the doorknob as leverage, Jason manages to pull himself to his feet. Hopping over to the light switch, he flips it. To his surprise, they actually turn on. When he sees his surroundings though, he wishes they hadn't. The floor is a wave of black and red. Crawling over each other, the spiders flow in and out of the now wide-open window. Jason watches, hope slowly draining, as a baby-sized, white sack is dragged up the wall. Just before the sack disappears over the sill, he catches a glimpse of a little finger poking through the webbing.

Jason's gentle sobbing only increases when he turns his attention to the other side of the room. Beverly is resting in the chair, at least what's left of her is. She rocks back and forth as the spiders continue to mutilate her body. It appears to Jason that both of her legs have been chewed off at the knee. Jagged flesh hangs where they were removed. One of her arms is also missing and numerous spiders seem to be swarming around the other.

He watches in horror as his theory is confirmed. They quickly chew right through her skin, dislocating humerus from scapula, and begin wrapping it up in a neat, little silky package. Once the sack is completed, it is dragged across the floor, up the wall and into the darkness beyond. Another group moves up her body, before coming together in the shape of a necklace. Red spots start to form. Blood spurts forth, spraying the wall and running down to join the growing puddle beneath the chair. Vomit starts to rise in Jason's throat as Beverly's head tilts forward and then topples to the floor at his feet; her eyes are open, staring blankly in his direction. The monsters begin wrapping it as well, crawling over her eyes and through her open mouth in the process. As before, when they are finished, it is dragged through the open window. This continues until the only thing left of Beverly is the red stain covering the hardwood floor.

Trembling, his back pressed firmly against the door, Jason swallows. *At least it's over.* His relief quickly dissipates when the spiders don't leave, but instead turn their attention to him. A swarm starts to gather at his feet, making their way up his legs. He begins hopping around the room, but trying to shake them off is useless. His muffled screams echo through the bungalow as their fangs sink into his flesh.

As the attack continues, he starts to lose control of his legs and allows himself to slide, with his back against the wall, to the floor. They chew through the ropes binding his legs, not that it does him any good now. Jason watches, thankful to have lost all feeling below the waist, as they gnaw clean through his left knee. He begins laughing hysterically, losing all touch with reality, as the same happens with his right.

Paralysis continues. Sensation leaves both arms and the laughter fades as his face goes numb. The spiders, working together, continue to dismember him. One group takes the right while the other takes the left and at the same time, both arms drop. Wrapped in webbing, they are taken. Another swarm scales his chest. Unable to look away, Jason welcomes what he knows is coming.

The jarring sound of furniture being dragged breaks the silence as the last part is bound in silky thread. The nursery door swings open, the dark figure filling the frame. Following the remaining spiders through the open window, they vanish into the night.

Chapter 20

"Hey!" Amy shouts from her tanning position by the poolside. "Watch it!"

Adam, ignoring her, uses the green, foam noodle to spray her again. She screams, leaping from the lounger and covering herself with a nearby towel. Laughing, I toss the beach ball into the air, preparing to serve it over the net to Luke. Missing, it splashes into the water beside me. Brandon and Devon race into the backyard, Max and Zoey yapping at their heels. As they are about to cannonball into the pool, my mother calls down to us from the deck above. "Who wants cake?"

A three tier masterpiece towers on the table before her. I've never seen anything like it. Decorated spectacularly, right down to the smallest detail, it's like one of those cakes that people pay thousands for on the reality shows.

Without skipping a beat, everyone shouts, "We do!"

I climb out of the pool, shivering, as a cool breeze begins to blow. Luke, following me, selects one of the towels waiting on a plastic patio chair and drapes it over my shoulders. Brandon and Devon race past us, charging up the stairs of the deck, the dogs at their sides. We all take our seats around the large, wooden table which is dwarfed by the cake upon it. My mother lights the candles while happy birthday is brutally sung by the group. Suddenly I feel like I'm five again.

While staring into the flickering flames before me, I notice the cake start to pulsate. Maybe I'm just imagining it. Luke tells me to make a wish as I take a deep breath and blow, surprisingly extinguishing every last one. When I finish removing the final candle, my mother passes me a large, steel knife and paper plate. The birthday girl gets to cut the first slice.

I bring the large knife down, piercing the cake. It bursts open, pink frosting splattering all of us. I stand, still wielding the knife, stunned. It isn't until the screaming starts that I see the spiders. With their red and black markings, they look like the one from the falls. I feel a tickling sensation across my forehead and realize they are crawling over my face and through my hair. Frozen with fear, the knife drops from my hand as I watch the horror unfold around me. The dogs shake furiously while biting at the spiders coating them. They only remove chunks of their own fur.

The screams intensify when the spiders begin sinking their fangs into flesh. Luke tries to escape, only to trip on the steps and break his neck, dying instantly. His head is left at an odd angle. Amy, stumbling down the stairs, trips over Luke. She falls into the pool, cracking her head against the side. Her lifeless body floats face down across the water. Brandon and Devon both lie unconscious on the deck, spiders feeding on their unmoving bodies.

Although I witness a couple crawl into Brandon's gaping mouth, my hopes are raised when I see his chest move. The feeling doesn't last long as moments later his chest bursts open, spider after spider crawling from within. My mother, still screaming, now has the knife in hand and is using it to swat at the spiders covering her. Unfortunately, she only succeeds in slicing herself with every swipe of the knife. This continues until she ends up fainting. A pool of blood gathers around her body, oozing from her open wounds.

Finally able to move, I race to my mother's side. Before I can catch myself, I slip in her blood and land on my back, staring up at the roof. Pain shooting from head to toe, I watch as a single spider descends towards my face. It gets closer and closer, its eight legs reaching out to me. I try to scream but nothing escapes my lips. It drops and-

DING DONG

The doorbell wakes me from my nightmare, drenched with sweat and covered by damp sheets. The awful dream felt so real. That's the last time I eat right before bed. Checking the phone on the nightstand, I discover it is already nine thirty. Rolling out of bed, I throw on some clean clothes and toss my sheets in the hamper.

"Lily," My mother calls as I enter the hallway. "You have visitors!"

Reaching the top of the stairs, I look down to see Amy and Adam standing in the front foyer with towels over their shoulders and bags at their feet.

"Happy Birthday!" They exclaim simultaneously, as if it was rehearsed.

When I meet them at the bottom of the stairs they sandwich me in a giant hug. Eventually they allow me to breathe and I lead them through the house to the backyard. Reminding me of my dream, the sight of the umbrella covered table positioned on the deck causes me to shudder. Adam and Amy add their presents to the pile resting upon it.

The party is going to be smaller than I had hoped. Nobody else from school would come and even my friends, only an hour away in New York, were either unable or unwilling to make it. My mother said Brandon had to be involved and allowed him to invite Devon from next door. It surprised me when Chief Wright agreed to let his son come. Mary said she might even stop by; she did help plan the party after all.

We are setting up the water volleyball net across the pool when the cordless phone begins ringing somewhere inside. It rings once, twice and then stops. With the net in place, Amy and I assign Adam the job of inflating a multi-colored beach ball.

"You're full of hot air anyway." Amy jokes, tossing the deflated ball to Adam. "You might as well use it."

"Lily, it's for you." My mother appears on the deck above us, portable phone in hand.

"Who is it?" I ask, heading up the stairs.

With a look of annoyance, she passes me the phone. "It's your father."

Chapter 21

"**H**appy Birthday!" My father exclaims so loud that I have to hold the phone away from my ear. He then asks, in the sweetest voice I've ever heard pass his lips, "How's my little princess?"

"Thanks Dad," I reply, frustration seeping in. "But I'm eighteen now. I'm not a little girl anymore"

"You'll always be my little girl." He says, taking a line straight out of some sappy movie.

And you'll always be the father that walked out on his children, I think to myself. How could he just up and leave us, for his secretary no less. How stereotypical is that? It's not like it happened over a period of time either. During breakfast, one Sunday morning, he told us he was moving out. The divorce followed shortly after.

Breaking the awkward silence, my father says, "I haven't told your mother yet, but..." He pauses briefly as if unsure of how to say the words. "Nicole and I are getting married."

"WHAT?" I shout into the receiver, nearly dropping it. Did he really just say what I think he did? My father remains silent on the other end, allowing me to take it in. Moments pass while I try to process this new information. Then, after taking a couple deep breaths, I ask, "Don't you think it's a little soon?"

"I know this might be hard for you to understand, Honey," He replies. "But Nicole and I do love each other. We want to share our day with you and Brandon. We are having a winter wedding and we want you guys to be there."

I don't know what to say. Part of me misses him and would love to be there, but the other half is still pissed and never wants to see him again. I want him to be happy, with my mother, not Nicole. Unable to give him a definite answer, I sidestep and reply with, "I'll have to think about it."

"OK... I understand. I hope you decide to come." He says, a slight hint of disappointment in his voice. "I love you... Princess."

I hang up without reply. Leaving the phone on the counter, I head back outside to find Adam and Amy already in the pool, passing the inflatable ball back and forth over the net. Zoey, watching intently, moves in time with the ball, waiting to get her paws on it. My mother lounges on a chair by the pool side, her face half hidden behind a romance novel. When she notices me, she lowers the book and asks, "So what did your father want?"

"Just wanted to say happy birthday," I answer, not wanting to upset her. She'll find out soon enough anyway. "That's all."

Zoey's sudden barking startles everyone. She darts off towards the front gate as it squeaks open. Max shoots between Luke's dark blue swim trunks, nearly knocking him to the ground. The dogs greet each other in their way while Luke, gift in hand, closes the gate. When he joins us by the pool, I introduce him to my mother. Following some awkward small talk, she pats me approvingly on the shoulder and takes the present from Luke. So far so good. She ascends the steps, leaves the gift on the table and enters the kitchen.

Brandon and Devon appear at the side of the house, bathing suits on and towels hanging off their shoulders. They start to cross the yard calmly, but the devilish grins on their faces tell me something is up. I'm trying to figure out what that something is when they drop their towels and race towards the pool. Before I have a chance to move, they cannonball in. The resulting splashes are not huge, but they are enough to soak both me and Luke. Apparently we were standing to close to the danger zone.

After a good laugh, Adam and Amy repay the pranksters with some splashes of their own, chasing them out of the water. Retrieving their towels, Brandon and Devon saunter off. After changing out of my wet clothes and into my two-piece, I return to the pool where Amy insists on a game of water volleyball. Boys against girls. Adam seems reluctant at first, but after some coaxing he goes along with it. He acts childish throughout the whole game though. Adam constantly dives in front of Luke whenever the ball comes near; he doesn't allow Luke to do anything. At least Luke acts like the bigger man, brushing it off. When all is said and done, guess who won. The girls of course!

I hear a door slide open and then voices singing, "Happy birthday to you." My mother appears on the deck above us, Mary next to her with a cake in hand. Everyone around me joins in. Even the dogs begin barking, wanting to be included. By the time the song ends, my face has turned a bright red. My mother then holds up a large knife for all to see. Grisly images from my nightmare flash through my mind as she asks, "Who wants cake?"

At the mention of cake, I hear and then see Brandon and Devon appear behind Mary on the deck. Scrambling out of the pool, we grab our towels and climb the wooden stairs. My mother pulls back a chair and I take the seat at the head of the table. The cake in front of me is one layer, covered in vanilla icing and has the words Happy 18th Birthday Lily piped across it in pink. Eighteen lit candles flicker around the edges. My mother, now sitting next to me, leans over and tells me to make a wish. I take a deep breath and manage to blow out every single candle. The table erupts in cheers as the knife is passed to me. I lift it into the air, my hand shaking terribly. With my eyes closed, I slowly bring the quivering knife down and cut into the cake. I'm relieved when it doesn't explode.

Opening my eyes, I pull the knife back and immediately recognize the dark tint. Red velvet, my favorite. My mouth waters as I pass slice after slice around the table. Once everyone has their own little slice of heaven, I cut a large piece for myself, put the knife down and dig in. As delicious as the cake is, three plates later my stomach tells me it has had enough. Moving onto presents, I open a crudely wrapped CD from Adam and a bottle of perfume from Amy. It's the thought that counts. The box Luke brought with him contains a beautiful sterling silver bracelet which I imagine must have cost him a pretty penny. I immediately place it around my wrist. Opening my mother's gift last, I find a heart shaped locket attached to a chain. Gently pulling it open reveals two photos, my mother and me.

"It's to show that no matter what happens," She turns to me, her voice cracking. "I love you and will always be with you."

My eyes start to swell as I stand and wrap my arms around her, squeezing her tight. Wiping my eyes, I thank everybody for their gifts and suggest heading back to the pool. Brandon and Devon take off like a shot, leaping down the stairs two at a time. Adam sneaks up behind Amy, snaps the back strap of her black bikini top and, laughing, races towards the pool. Amy, appearing furious, chases after him. I begin to prepare a playlist of songs on my phone, planning to use it as our stereo, while my mother and Mary clear the table. The moment they disappear inside with handfuls of dishes, Luke pulls me aside. My wish comes true when he whispers the words, "How would you like to go out sometime?"

Chapter 22

Who saw me? What did they see? Who left the note? Ever since finding that blank envelope stashed in his mailbox, these thoughts have been floating around Mr. Walker's worried mind. His weekend was awful. He spent every waking moment trying to figure out the person's identity. Due to a sudden onset of insomnia, those waking moments have been non-stop. With Adam busy most of the weekend, there was plenty of time to think. The only interruption was when his elderly neighbor knocked on the door Sunday afternoon, checking up on him as she often does.

"Yoo hoo, Earth to Vince."

Blinking, Mr. Walker looks up. Judy stands next to him in the crowded teacher's lounge, waving her hand in front of his face. When they make eye contact, she realizes he has finally returned to reality. She stops waving, places a bag on the round table and takes the seat next to him.

Opening the bag, Judy withdraws a sandwich covered in plastic wrap. "What's on your mind?" She peels away the last piece of plastic from her sliced, egg salad sandwich and takes a bite.

"It's none of your business!" Mr. Walker snaps.

Judy freezes in place, sandwich hanging from the corner of her mouth, shocked at his sudden outburst. Everyone turns in their direction as the room becomes awkwardly silent.

"Well now," Judy says, placing the sandwich back on the table. "I was only trying to make conversation."

"I know... I'm sorry." Mr. Walker covers both eyes, inhales deeply and runs his hands down over his cheeks. Before continuing, he lets the air out in one long exhale. "I shouldn't have yelled at you. I haven't been getting much sleep lately." Then turning to the rest of the room he says, "Sorry everyone."

The noise starts to pick up again as previous conversations resume. Mr. Walker rests his forehead on the table, wishing the day would hurry up and come to an end. Judy places one hand on the back of his neck, gently massaging, while continuing to eat with the other.

A few minutes pass before Mr. Walker sits back in his chair and takes a swig of his now cold coffee. The last thing he needs is to pass out from exhaustion during his afternoon classes.

"You know," Judy removes a juice box from the bag. Inserting the straw, she seductively circles it with her tongue. "If you need help sleeping, I know something that will tire you out."

They both laugh, although Mr. Walker has the sneaking suspicion that Judy would follow through without a second thought. This certainly isn't the first time she has jokingly suggested something of that nature.

Pushing back his chair, Mr. Walker approaches the sink and dumps the remains of his coffee, watching it spiral down the drain. He then refills his mug with fresh caffeine and leaves the lounge, Judy following closely behind.

"Remember what I said." Judy says, winking. "Open invitation."

Laughing again, they head in their opposing directions. As Judy starts back towards the office, Mr. Walker turns and watches, wondering what it would be like to take her up on her offer. Admiring the way her hips sway as she glides down the hall, he decides it would be amazing.

Back in his currently empty, semi-dark classroom, Mr. Walker plops down on his chair, places his mug on the desk and closes his eyes. He is beginning to enjoy the quiet when the warning bell rings, marking the end of lunch. As his students noisily enter the classroom, a dull pain starts to build behind his right eye. After discretely popping a couple pills, trying to catch the headache before it escalates, he turns and begins third period.

As with his morning classes, he spends most of the period focusing on his student's faces, watching for a sign that will let him know who left the note. If the culprit is in this class however, they aren't giving themselves away.

Mr. Walker is thankful when the class finally comes to an end. His whole head throbs, the pills not doing their job. As the students gather their things and leave, he feels relieved in knowing that there is only one class left. He finishes clearing the blackboard when the faint scent of marijuana fills his nostrils.

He is unsurprised to see Nathan Reid walk past him, towards his seat at the back of the room. Nathan drops into his chair, places his feet on the desktop, looks at Mr. Walker with his bloodshot eyes and nods.

"Nathan, get your feet off the desk." Mr. Walker says as the classroom starts to fill. "Other people sit there too you know."

"Sure thing Mr. W." His feet hit the floor with an echoing thud. "Whatever you say." Rubbing his temples, Mr. Walker begins his final class. There are no other disruptions and when the bell rings everyone races out, anxious to escape the confines of the school walls; everyone except for Nathan.

While Mr. Walker energetically packs his briefcase, looking forward to leaving as well, Nathan saunters up to his desk. With his backpack over his shoulders, he places his hands on the desktop and leans in close. The smell of marijuana emanates from him.

"Did you get my note?" He whispers.

"That was you!" Mr. Walker blurts out. A stack of papers falls from his hands, scattering around his feet.

"Oh it was me alright Mr. W." A grin appears on Nathan's face as he watches Mr. Walker scramble to collect the pages. "I saw everything. But you couldn't see me could you?" He doesn't wait for a reply. "Of course not! You know that large willow tree at the edge of the parking lot? When you're up high enough, it gives the perfect cover. I can see the whole lot, and nobody ever thinks to look up." He shakes his head in mock disappointment. "So there I am, enjoying my lunchtime ritual when I spot you exit the back door of the school and casually stroll across the parking lot, baseball bat in hand. I can only imagine where you got that. You look around, checking to see if anyone is watching, not noticing me up above. Then you start laying into that jock's car." Nathan swings an invisible bat. "I must admit I was shocked. And then when you pulled out the knife and started slashing his tires. Wow!" His eyes light up as he replays it in his mind. "You've got a dark side don't you Mr. W?"

"OK Nathan," Mr. Walker says, picking up the final sheet and placing the stack in his briefcase. "What do you want?"

"Nothing much, you're just going to pass me with flying colors. During class, if I even decide to come, I'll be relaxing with my feet up, nothing more. No homework or labs. And when I fail every test, your red little marker will give it an A. It's either that or I go to the cops." Nathan takes a step back and shrugs. "Your choice. From what I understand, they currently think the new girl is to blame. How could you let a student take the fall for you?"

"Th... that wasn't the plan. I di... didn't intend for her to be accused."

"So do we have a deal?" Nathan sticks out his hand, ignoring Mr. Walker's attempt at an explanation.

"OK Nathan, I'll-"

"Ready to go Dad?"

They both turn to see Adam standing in the doorway, school bag in hand. Nathan raises his outstretched arm, running his hand through his hair.

"Yeah." Looking back at Nathan, Mr. Walker nods. "We're done here."

Nathan winks and leaves the room, pushing his way past Adam on the way out.

"What was that about?" Adam asks.

With sealed briefcase in one hand, Mr. Walker grabs his mug with the other and places his arm around

Adam's shoulders. "Don't worry about it." He turns off the lights as they leave the room. "Let's go home."

Chapter 23

The afternoon sun strikes my hair, causing it to glisten in the mirror. Sitting alone in my bedroom, brush in hand, my mind lingers on Luke. He couldn't wait to take me out and somehow convinced my mother to allow our first date to happen on a Monday. A school night! She actually seemed happy about it. Her only request was that we be home early.

Now, my only concern is what to wear. Placing the brush on the dresser, I search through the closet. I settle on a pair of black pants and a blue blouse, wanting to be casual and not too girly. Luke doesn't seem the type that would like that anyway. Maybe it's just because he's older, but Luke seems more mature than any other guy I've had the pleasure of meeting. I can't believe how lucky I am to have met him, and so early after moving here. I keep waiting for the other shoe to drop.

The pants are a little snug, but I manage to get them on. I begin slipping into the blouse when I hear, "Lily and Luke sitting in a tree..."

After quickly pulling the blouse over my body, I turn to see Brandon standing in my doorway, Zoey at his side.

"Brandon! Get out!"

I slam the door shut, nearly hitting the tongue he has aimed in my direction. How long was he standing there? Gross! I push that thought from my mind and return to the mirror. Not too bad if I do say so myself. Not too much skin, and not too little. Opening the small, wooden jewelry box on my dresser, I pick up the final pieces to my wardrobe. The locket feels cool as it rests against my chest. I just finish with the clasp when my mother calls up to me, "Lily!"

I slide the bracelet around my wrist before taking one last look in the mirror. I open the door and almost run over Zoey. Seriously? Brandon is still outside my door, leaning against the wall.

"So what are you going to do?" Brandon starts as soon as I leave the room. "Where are you guys going?" He pauses before continuing in a sly voice. "Are you gonna make out?"

"Oh my god Brandon!" My shouting causes Zoey to start barking. Brandon, once again being overdramatic, falls to the floor laughing. I head for the stairs, leaving him on the carpet where Zoey seems content with washing his face.

Luke and my mother are standing together by the front door. I'm glad I chose to go casual. Luke is dressed in a pair of jeans and a black, button down shirt, collar up. His hands are behind his back, trying to hide a bouquet of roses which are too large to conceal.

"For my lady", he says, holding them out to me as I descend.

I take the roses and carry them in my arms the way you would a new born child. A camera appears in my mother's hand. Where was she hiding that?

"OK you two, get close, I want a picture." She says, raising the camera while watching the screen on back. "Lily, hold up the roses, I want them in the picture. Smile" There is a flash and I'm momentarily blinded. "So Luke, where are you two going tonight?" As my vision gradually clears, I watch my mother turn off the digital camera and place it in her back pocket.

"I thought we'd go for an early dinner at this lovely little restaurant downtown." He replies. "Then we're going to see a movie."

"That sounds nice. Just don't be too late." She reminds us while I pass her my bouquet. "It is a school night after all."

When we begin to hear exaggerated kissing sounds coming from upstairs, we take it as our cue to leave. Luke has a cramped, two-seater parked in the driveway. I'm amazed that we both fit into it. The car comes to life with the turn of the key and rattles as we back out of the driveway. My mother watches intently from the front porch.

"Are you sure we're going to make it there alive?" I joke as the rattling continues.

"Are you insulting old clunky?" Luke sticks out his lower lip.

Laughing, I wave to my mother as we drive away.

The entrance to The Cellar is hidden down an alley in the middle of town. The only signage is a sandwich board with a large red arrow and the name in block letters. As we approach a short flight of stone steps, my first thought is run, run now! After crossing the threshold though, my opinion does a complete reversal. It is beautiful and quite romantic. Even though it is afternoon and the sun is still shining, the restaurant is dimly lit. Some might refer to it as mood lighting. Wood paneling covers the surrounding walls. All the tables are fashioned with a red tablecloth and candle.

Bottles line the wall behind a bar at the opposite side of the room. Wine glasses hang from above and five red-cushioned stools sit before it, three of them filled. The young bartender appears to be showing off for one of the female customers, spinning a bottle in each hand before pouring her drink.

When our hostess appears, menus in hand, she stops dead in her tracks.

"Vanessa," Luke says. "I didn't realize you worked here."

"Sure." She mumbles. "Follow me."

Vanessa leads us to a quiet corner booth where she slaps the menus onto the table and walks away.

"I take it she's not your biggest fan?" I ask, sliding into the booth.

"Not since we broke up." Luke positions himself across from me, the small candle lighting the area between us.

I nod. "Well, other than her, this place is beautiful."

"Yeah, and not many people know about it." Luke reaches across the table and takes my hand in his. "Only the lucky ones."

After a few minutes, Vanessa returns to take our orders. "What do you want?" She asks, bitterness dominating her voice. Luke gives her his order before she turns to me, glaring. "And you?" She scribbles down my order and scurries away. What was that all about? I have so many questions about her but I decide tonight probably isn't the best time.

Luke and I are enjoying our time alone when Vanessa returns with our meals. She drops the plates onto the table without making eye contact and again rushes off. Luke has to assure me the food is safe before I take a bite. The awkwardness continues when we finish eating and she drops off the check. Luke pays, not leaving a tip.

As nice as the restaurant is, I'm overjoyed when we enter the alley. Arriving on the sidewalk, hand in hand, we decide to walk the block to the theater. The sun is beginning to set over the tree tops. Streaks of red paint the sky. We pass numerous people, but at the moment the only person in my world is Luke.

For a Monday evening, the theater is rather busy. I guess when you live in a small town like this there isn't much else to do. As we approach a growing line, I begin to wonder how old this place is. The word THEATER stands out prominently on a vertical sign along the front of the building and there is actually a ticket booth at the front entrance. A bright sign above the booth displays the three films currently playing and their show times. When we reach the head of the line, Luke and I walk up to the plump man behind the glass.

Tickets in hand, we step through the doors and into a room filled with the clamor of conversation. As Luke leads me through the crowd towards the concession stand, we pass an arcade with various video games, pinball machines and even an air hockey table. While we stand in line for our overpriced snacks, I notice that none of the theaters have doors. Instead, each is closed off with a red velvet curtain. Classy.

A pimply, squeaky-voiced teen serves us our large popcorn and soft drinks. We try hard not to laugh every time he speaks.

"Would you like butter on that?" He asks, his voice cracking on the word butter.

"Yes, please" We manage to say, stifling our laughter.

The young man standing next to theater three holds the curtain open for us after checking our tickets. Trailers play as we find a couple empty seats near the wall. We settle in with our drinks and popcorn. The girl on screen continues to spin while her dress goes up in flames.

When the trailers come to an end, Luke pulls the clichéd move of yawning and placing his arm around my shoulders. I don't try to stop it and instead lean into him as the lights start to dim.

Chapter 24

Cheers fill the theater as the typical housewife blows up a supermarket before casually driving away. Luke wasn't sure he would like the film, but now he is glad he chose it. The only thing he is regretting is the large cola. Feeling the urge, he removes his arm from around Lily's shoulders.

"I've got to use the washroom." He says, standing. "I'll be right back."

"OK... But don't be too long." Lily wraps her arms around herself and pretends to shiver. "I might get cold."

Leaving Lily, her sly grin, and the rest of the audience behind, Luke pushes his way through the velvet curtain. With all three movies playing, the lobby is nearly vacant. Luke passes the concession stand, where Squeaks is cleaning the popcorn machine, and marches straight for the washrooms along the far wall. As he reaches for the door to the men's room, he hears someone charging towards him.

The portly man from the ticket booth passes Luke, pushing his way into the one person restroom. "I shouldn't have had those burritos!" The man says as he slams the door shut behind him. The lock clicks into place leaving Luke stranded and waiting, although he is unsure if he wants to use the washroom after what he just heard.

When the grunting starts, Luke decides standing next to the door is no longer an option. He wanders over to the arcade where a couple of older kids are using the air hockey table. They challenge Luke to a game, which he declines.

"Chicken!" They taunt Luke, unsuccessfully.

He examines the other games filling the arcade while periodically checking the washroom. Racing games, fighting games, a couple old pinball machines and...The Claw. Peering through the stained acrylic glass, Luke thinks back on the hours he spent in front of this machine. Whether he was skipping class or stopping in after school, The Claw continued to eat quarter after quarter. Even though winning was rare, he had still returned, more determined than ever.

Snuggled in amongst the other plush characters rests a cute, pink bear with round, black eyes and a red heart covering its chest. Intent on winning it for Lily, Luke reaches into his pocket, pulls out four quarters and slides them into the coin slot. His years of practice pay off as he maneuvers The Claw over the bear and manages to grasp it by one of its pink fluffy ears. The Claw is air-lifting its prize across the sea of stuffed animals when an ear splitting scream roars through the lobby. Startled, Luke bumps the machine causing the little bear to drop from The Claw's grasp. It lands on the plastic divider separating winners from losers before toppling over into the return chute. When another scream rips through the lobby though, Luke forgets all about the toy.

The air hockey game has come to an abrupt halt. The kids stand huddled, staring in the direction of the washroom.

"You guys stay here." Luke says, passing them. "I'll see what's going on."

One of them manages to stammer, "OK M-Mister."

Squeaks approaches the washroom and knocks on the wooden door.

"Rob!" He calls out. "Are you OK in there? Rob?"

A growing crowd of onlookers starts to surround the scene. People continue to flow out of the nearest theater. Receiving no reply, Squeaks tries the door. Locked. He then rams it with his shoulder. His scrawny body does nothing.

Pushing his way through young and old, Luke places a hand on Squeaks' arm. "Let me give it a try." Obliging, Squeaks steps back into the murmur of the crowd. When Luke raises his hand, the room falls silent. He presses his ear against the door. A faint shuffling can be heard, nothing more.

"Rob... Are you OK?" No answer. "Rob, if you can hear me, stay away from the door."

With handle in hand, Luke slams his body against the door. The sound of wood cracking echoes through the lobby. Taking a deep breath and a step back, he hits the door again with all his weight. The lock breaks free of the wooden frame and the door flies open.

The crowd gasps. A woman screams while another weeps. Parents turn their children away. Someone even vomits. The scene is ghastly. Luke can't help but gag. Against the wall of the washroom, Rob lies in a growing puddle of red and brown.

The stench is nauseating. Rob's headless torso sits propped against the blood streaked wall. Both legs are gone and one arm is missing. Following the smears of blood along the white tile floor, Luke finds the other arm. A cluster of spiders are slowly dragging the silken wrapped arm up the wall towards a vent near the ceiling. He watches as they disappear into the darkness of the air shaft.

Fighting the urge to vomit, Luke takes another look at Rob and notices the slight rise and fall of his chest. *There's no way he could still be alive. How could he still be breathing?* Then it dawns on him.

"Everyone get back!"

Grabbing hold of the handle again, Luke pulls the washroom door closed as Rob's chest explodes.

Chapter 25

What's taking Luke so long? He should have been back by now. I'm still sitting alone in the dark theater, anxiously spinning my locket between my fingers. Watching this movie has become impossible, especially with all the screams coming from the movie playing in the neighboring theater. They really should invest in some sound proof doors.

I pick up my soda and bring the straw to my lips as another loud shriek fills the theater. The lid pops off when my hands clench the paper cup. Soda splashes forth, creating a sticky mess. The screaming continues. People in the audience begin to look annoyed. A large man, a few rows ahead of me, stands up and storms out of the theater. Following in his footsteps, I put down the soda and make my way past the other audience members. Popcorn crunches beneath my feet as I approach the closed curtain.

I realize the screams are real when I push through the red velvet and happen upon a large crowd. A woman on her knees continues to scream, over and over again. A man brushes past me, followed closely by a young woman and child. They make a bee line for the exit. On a padded bench along the wall sits a young boy with his head in his hands. A puddle of what appears to be vomit surrounds his sneakers. I notice Squeaks behind the concession stand talking into a cell phone with his back to the group. The rest of the onlookers are huddled around the washroom, mumbling loudly to each other.

After quickly scanning the remainder of the lobby, my heart starts to race. Luke is nowhere in sight. Was he injured... or worse? What happened?

"Luke?" I scream for him as I plunge into the swarm of people, forcing my way forward. It's like trying to push through a brick wall. These people really don't want to budge. A small gap opens and I catch a glimpse of Luke standing only a few feet away, unharmed. Breathing a sigh of relief, I begin to squeeze through the opening. As I get closer Luke notices me. His eyes light up at first, but that look is quickly replaced by worry and concern.

"Lily! You have to get back." He says. "It isn't sa-"

Suddenly someone shifts, the gap opens, and I stumble forward. Unable to catch myself, I collide with Luke. We both fall through the bathroom door and slide across the tile floor, coming to a stop in a dark pool of blood. As my blouse absorbs its surroundings, the dampness feels cool against my skin. I want to scream, but nothing comes out. Luke scrambles to his feet and quickly pulls me to mine. When we turn to leave, a shimmer catches my eye. A small silver canister sits, barely visible, behind the toilet.

"Lily, don't touch anyth-"

It's too late. The canister is already in my hands. As I examine it, I discover it has some kind of electronic device attached to the top.

Luke touches my hand. "Let's get out of here."

I nod and drop the canister back into its hiding place. With my hand in his, Luke leads me from that horrible room. While crossing back into the lobby, I hear him mutter under his breath, "They took the whole body?"

"Who?... Luke?...What happened?" Unresponsive, he continues to lead us towards the bench farthest from the scene. "Just tell me." I say. "I'll find out eventually anyway."

He sits and motions for me to take a seat next to him. "Rob, the guy from the ticket booth, ran into the washroom..." He starts.

"Go on." I urge.

"He was killed by damn spiders Lily!"

"Spiders?... What are you talking about Luke?"

"Hundreds of little spiders. His chest exploded right in front of me."

I'm suddenly reminded of my dream and all I manage to utter is, "It's actually happening."

The sirens bring me back and I slowly close my gaping mouth. They continue to get louder and then I see the flashing lights. Officers flow through the front doors, guns raised. I guess they didn't get the memo. The murderers are long gone. And they were spiders!

My favorite police chief brings up the rear and is met by Squeaks. After a brief discussion, during which Squeaks points directly at Luke, Chief Wright speaks into the radio attached to his shirt. The officers begin lowering their guns. He then pulls out a cell phone, makes a quick call, tucks the phone away and heads in our direction. Great, here we go again.

"So, I hear you found the body." Chief Wright says, getting straight to the point. "Before it disappeared?" Luke nods and details the night's events. As I listen, I can't help but imagine what it must have been like. When I visibly shudder, the Chief turns to me. "Hello again Ms. Crawford. Why am I not surprised to see you here?" He says, condescending as always. "Why do bad things always seem to happen when you're around?"

"Chief?" A man calls out as he enters the theater. The gray jumpsuit he wears has the words Ed's Extermination printed over the right breast and the name Ed sewn over the left. Chief Wright leaves Luke and I standing there, shocked at his accusation. Clenching my jaw, I watch him greet Ed the exterminator and manage to catch the words "Not another one" escape Ed's lips.

"Chief, I think we've found something!"

We turn in the direction of the shouting. A young officer sporting a goatee waits by the washroom door. Chief Wright dons a pair of gloves and follows him into the now taped off crime scene. My heart skips a beat when he emerges with two items in his gloved hands. He places the silver canister into an evidence bag and my open locket into another. An officer carries the bags away while Chief Wright approaches us. He points a gloved finger at Luke. "Stop by the station to make an official statement. And Ms. Crawford," His steely glare falls upon me. "Don't think about leaving town."

Chapter 26

The moon shines high above as Nathan pushes his way through the overgrowth. With the only camera in the cemetery pointed directly at the main gate, entering over the fence has become the new normal. He has been meeting his friends here for years and has learned to move amongst the shadows.

Reaching the metal picket fence, he takes the backpack from his shoulders and tosses it over, after giving it a quick kiss and wishing it a safe landing. He wouldn't want anything to happen to his Fun Bag, named after those which he finds so enticing, even though it is used for a different purpose. Contained within is a bottle of vodka, courtesy of his parent's liquor cabinet, and a large bag of marijuana.

When his Fun Bag lands softly on the other side, Nathan starts climbing. With one leg over, he is in his most feared location. One wrong move could mean immense pain and no future children. He carefully lifts his other leg up and over. When he jumps, Nathan lands on his feet, drops to the ground and rolls to a stop in a patch of grass.

The sudden clapping lets him know he's not alone. Josh steps into view. "Nice landing." He says while laughing. "A perfect score!" Reaching down, he helps Nathan to his feet. "You've got a little something." Josh gently brushes a stray leaf from Nathan's hair.

"Thanks, but I'm pretty sure I could have got that." Nathan says, feeling uncomfortable. Collecting his bag, he continues deeper into the cemetery with Josh in tow.

As he moves through the darkness of the surrounding trees, a small glimmer of light appears in the distance. Inching closer, Nathan can make out movement. In the glow of a few small candles, Kyle and Wade sit between a group of tombstones, blowing smoke into the night sky. A branch snaps beneath Nathan's foot as he nears the clearing. Prepared to bolt, Kyle and Wade leap to their feet. The joint is dropped and crushed.

"Calm down guys." Nathan says, emerging with Josh by his side. "It's just us."

"What took you guys so long?" Kyle asks, settling back into his place against one of the cracked tombstones. "Making out in there?"

Nathan tells him to shove it while Josh's face turns red.

"I hope you remembered the stuff." Wade says, taking a seat across from Kyle.

"Of course." Nathan holds up his bag for all to see. "Have I ever let you down?" Unzipping it, he pulls out the bag of marijuana and tosses it to Wade. Grabbing the bottle of vodka, he twists off the top. After taking a swig, Nathan passes the bottle to Josh and plops down next to Kyle. Pulling a lighter from his pocket, he hands it to Wade who lights a now packed glass pipe.

"So how did your little talk with Walker go?" Josh asks before taking a sip from the bottle and passing it to Kyle.

"Let's just say the rest of the year is going to be smooth sailing." Nathan takes the pipe and lighter from Wade. "No dropping out for me." He brings the pipe to his lips, lights it, and breathes in deeply. A trail of smoke slowly escapes as he then passes the pipe and lighter to Josh. "Not like the rest of you losers." Kyle punches Nathan square in the shoulder.

"I still can't believe he did that." Josh smiles, picturing Mr. Walker brandishing a baseball bat and swinging at a car repeatedly. "I wish I'd seen it."

The bottle, having made its rounds, returns to Nathan. "Just keep your mouth shut about it though." Holding the bottle in his lap, he looks around at the only group of people that have ever truly understood him. "If anyone else finds out then my whole plan goes to shit!"

"Don't worry man." The corner of Wade's mouth curls up in a sly grin. "Have we ever let you down?"

Josh ruffles Nathan's hair while passing the pipe and lighter to Kyle.

"So, now that you'll be passing with flying colors, what's the plan for after graduation?" Kyle asks, following a long inhale.

"You know, I haven't' really thought about it. I never thought I would graduate in the first place." Nathan takes another swig before passing the bottle to Josh. He stares up into the night sky, admiring the twinkling stars overhead. "Maybe I'll become a teacher."

Vodka erupts from Josh's lips. He continues to cough while the others laugh. He can just picture Nathan as a teacher. What would he teach? Getting high 101?

When Josh finally catches his breath, he hands the near empty bottle back to Nathan. "Just don't become some big shot and leave us behind." Josh says, placing a palm on Nathan's shoulder and softly squeezing. "OK?"

Nathan nods as he finishes the vodka. He then tosses the empty bottle into the darkness of the surrounding trees. Taking the pipe and lighter from Wade, Nathan enjoys one more long inhale. Another stream of smoke escapes, trailing towards the moon.

Nature comes calling as the alcohol starts to take effect. Standing, Nathan stumbles forward. He grabs the top of the nearest tombstone, knocking the lit candle into the dry grass. Wade quickly jumps to his feet.

"Careful man! You're going to start a fire!" After ensuring the candle is snuffed out, Wade turns and watches Nathan shuffle towards the trees. "Hey! Where are you going?"

"Gotta piss." Nathan calls over his shoulder. "I'll be right back."

Shuffling his way along, trying not to move too fast for fear of falling on his face, Nathan enters the shadows. Using the trees for support, Nathan stumbles further and further away from the group. Eventually they are nothing but specks in the distance. Feeling he has gone far enough, he selects one of the nearby trees. While using his right hand to lean against it, he unzips.

That's when the steel cracks against the back of his skull.

Chapter 27

Blinking, Nathan opens his eyes. His head throbs. Something warm trickles down the back of his neck. A warm wetness also covers his lower half. *Where am I? What happened?* His head is filled with fog; the memories just aren't coming.

Alone in the darkness, Nathan struggles to figure things out. He hears laughter in the distance and focuses his eyes on the direction of the sound. A glimmer of light outlines what looks like a tombstone. *The cemetery!* The dots finally connect. He was attacked! Someone struck him from behind. But who?

Nathan screams to his friends. "Help! I'm over here!"

It comes out faint and muffled. His eyes go wide. Trying again gets the same result. Nathan begins to realize there is something covering his mouth. Opening his mouth as wide as possible, he feels it pull on his skin. *Is that duct tape?* He tries reaching up to remove the tape. No such luck. Straining to move his arms only causes the rope securing them behind his back to burn into his wrists.

Propped against the trunk of a large tree, his heart starts racing. Knowing he has to escape, Nathan tries to stand. The rope digs into his ankles as he fails to separate his legs. *Shit!* Thoughts are bouncing around his brain when he hears footsteps approaching from his left.

They continue to get closer. In an attempt to attract attention, Nathan makes muffled shouts for help while slamming his legs against the leaf covered ground. The steps get louder and louder before stopping only a few feet away. Nathan continues to make as much noise as possible. Scouring the area, he is unable to see anyone.

It isn't until he looks up that he spots them. A pair of cold, unfeeling eyes stare back at him. All his hopes of rescue sink. Straining, he can just make out the shape of a person. They are dressed all in black, from the shoes on their feet to the mask over their face.

"What do you want?" Nathan screams at the dark figure before him. "Let me go!" Of course it all comes out muffled, but it makes him feel a little better. The dark figure doesn't seem to notice as they begin unzipping the front of their jacket. Reaching in with a black gloved hand, they pull out something silver. It appears to be an unlabeled can of spray paint.

What new horror is this? Nathan bends his knees as the dark figure zips back up. When they move within range, Nathan strikes out. He misses miserably as the dark figure easily sidesteps the kick. They stand watching with those cold eyes as if to say, "Are you done?" Feeling defeated, Nathan leans his head against the trunk of the tree.

Spray can in hand, the dark figure removes the cap, gives it a vigorous shake and again stands over Nathan. Aiming the nozzle in his direction, Nathan is sprayed from head to foot. *What the Hell!* The mist coats his face and drips from his chin. It feels cool against his chest as it soaks through his shirt.

After recapping the can, the dark figure returns it to the hidden compartment in their jacket. Finding a neighboring tree, they lean against it, cross their arms and watch. *You spray me with some gunk and watch? Pretty lame!* Nathan begins laughing to himself when he suddenly hears a scuffling noise ahead of him. Squinting, he watches as the ground comes to life. The leaf covered floor ripples as something moves beneath. A breeze blows through the trees, allowing the moon to light the area in front of him.

His eyes bulge when he sees hundreds of spiders crawling in his direction. The urge to flee takes hold. Nathan quickly flips onto his stomach and begins inching his way across the ground towards the light of the candles. The dark figure has so much faith in their little minions that they don't even budge.

Nathan wiggles and pushes himself forward with his toes. Believing he might actually escape, Nathan again tries screaming to his friends. Before anything can pass his lips, he is surprised by the tickling sensation moving up his leg. Nathan furiously whacks his legs against the ground until he feels the spider squish against his skin. His relief is short lived as two more take its place.

When they begin to bite, Nathan gives up crawling, rolls over and sits up. He feels more crush in the process. Hundreds continue to crawl towards him while the dark figure, still leaning against the tree, watches with those cold eyes. Exhausted, Nathan gives up. Closing his eyes, he lies back and lets the spiders engulf him.

Once the paralysis sets in and Nathan's body stops twitching, they set to work dismembering him. The spiders chew through his neck, droplets of blood running down his unmoving chest. When Nathan's head hits the ground, it is quickly wrapped in silky web and dragged away. Another group of spiders crawls into his now open neck.

The dark figure watches in silence and admiration. When Nathan's chest bursts open, numerous spiders crawl forth pulling organs with them. The heart, liver, stomach, and a kidney are dragged away. The dark figure is filled with pride as they observe a few spiders working together to remove the intestine.

Once all limbs have been removed, only one part remains. The spiders roll the hollow torso over and over again. When it is completely wrapped in web, they drag it off into the night. A single thought fills the dark figure's mind as they follow closely behind. *That's what I call teamwork.*

Chapter 28

"**I** think you should stay home today."

My mother leans against the kitchen counter, the aroma from her morning coffee filling the room. I breathe it in while sitting at the island with my bowl of cereal.

"I'm fine Mom." Unable to take it any longer, I get up, grab a cup and pour my own. "Don't worry."

I take a sip of the warm coffee. It's just what I needed.

"But after what happened, don't you think you should take some time to rest?" She continues. "It was quite an ordeal."

My mother is right about that. When someone goes out on a date they don't generally expect to get caught up in a murder investigation. I can only imagine what Luke is going through. Opening the door onto a headless, dismembered corpse. Spiders bursting from its chest. All the screams. I shudder thinking about it.

After leaving the theater, we had walked back to Luke's car in silence. He put on a strong front but it was obvious he was in shock. I was still furious with Chief Wright but also worried about how he would pin this on me. Especially since my locket was coated in blood. It wasn't until we were in the car with the engine running that I tried talking to Luke again. He remained tight lipped. The only sign of emotion was the single tear as we pulled away.

When we arrived at my house, Luke walked me to the door. I had insisted he come inside but he assured me he would be fine. Following a quick kiss on the cheek, Luke had driven away. All I could do was stand on the porch, watching his car shrink and then vanish.

My mother was waiting up for me, wanting to hear all about our first date. When I filled her in on the situation, she immediately transformed into Supermom. Out came the tissues and hot cocoa. We curled up on the living room sofa and talked for hours. It was wonderful being able to talk to her like that. I just wish Luke had been there. With the hot cocoa gone and the tissues depleted, we had called it a night.

"It was an ordeal, but I can't sit around here all day thinking about it. I need to be around my friends." I say, returning to my cereal. "I need a distraction."

"Fine, you can go." She stares past me. "I understand needing a distraction."

The explosion causes us both to jump. My mother spills her coffee on the tile floor.

"Brandon, turn it down!" She shouts to my brother in the next room.

Brandon and Zoey are engaged in their morning routine. Watching cartoons in the living room while eating dry cereal. Zoey follows him everywhere. Of course that could have something to do with Brandon constantly dropping food for her.

Noticing the time, I quickly down the rest of my cereal. After chugging my coffee, I grab my bag, say my goodbyes and rush out the door.

I find Amy at her locker, Adam by her side. Adam spots me and speeds over. When he drapes his arm around my shoulders, I place my hand on his.

"We can't keep doing this." I say, lifting his arm away. "I'm with Luke now. You know that. Besides, after what happened, everyone else will too." His head lowers, eyes focused on the floor. "Still friends?" I ask.

Adam nods while mumbling, "Of course."

"Oh my god!" Amy exclaims as we approach. "Are you OK? Your texts didn't do it justice. I saw it all on the news."

I give a brief retelling of last night's events.

"How could they think it was you?" Adam asks, finally raising his head.

"Well, they did find my locket." Their jaws drop. "I'm more worried about Luke right now though." I continue. "With his parents out of town, he's all alone."

"I'm sure he'll be fine." Adam mutters.

Before I can reply, the warning bell rings. The class is already full when we arrive. Mr. Walker stands at the front of the room, watching as we take our seats.

He is just about to explain our assignment for the day when the overhead system crackles to life. Principal Harris' monotone voice flows through the speakers. "This is a very important message. One of our students, Nathan Reid has been reported missing. He never returned home last night. His parents are understandably worried. If anyone has any information, no matter how small you think it may be, please let us know immediately. Thank you."

There is a moment of static and then the overhead system dies. The other students look at each other for a minute, then the comments start.

"He actually has parents?" Brittney, the head Snobette, asks. "And they care what happens to him?"

Someone in back says, "If anything happened to him, it's not like he didn't deserve it."

Another states, "He probably got so high he passed out somewhere."

"OK, that's enough." Mr. Walker says while clearing the blackboard. He then piles his notes back into his briefcase. "It's such a beautiful day. Let's have class outside."

Chapter 29

"Ewww! Gross!"

Amy uses her spoon to pick out the random pea that has managed to worm its way into her chocolate pudding. Adam and I watch in disgust as she digs it out and flings the chocolate covered pea across the cafeteria. It splatters against the white wall and slowly begins its decent to the floor. At least the mystery meatloaf isn't so bad. Although I don't think I want to know what the mystery is.

"I think we should try to figure out what's going on." I blurt out before filling my mouth with another chunk of meatloaf.

They stare at me with blank expressions. The plastic, chocolate covered spoon hangs from Amy's mouth. She slowly removes it while Adam returns to his own lunch.

"What do you mean exactly?" Amy asks.

"The murder of course!" I declare, dropping my fork onto the orange tray. "And now Nathan's missing? Do you think that's a coincidence?"

"Maybe." Amy replies with a shrug. "It wouldn't surprise me. Nathan lives by his own rules."

I never really knew Nathan, but from the stories I've heard, it is quite possible. "That may be so, but the police already think I'm involved." I state. "I'm not going to let them pin this on me."

"It sounds kind of dangerous." Adam, finished with his lunch, joins the conversation. "What if you get hurt... or worse?"

"Well," I stand and pick up my tray. "That's the chance I'm going to have to take." I turn to Amy. "You want to be a reporter right? Imagine if you were to solve this case. All doors would be open. Everyone would want you." I watch as her eyes light up at the idea.

"That's true..." Amy trails off.

"And Adam," I pause, thinking. "Well... we could use a bodyguard."

Amy laughs so hard I fear the milk she is drinking will shoot across the table. She manages to hold it in.

"So are we going to do this?" I ask, determined to clear my name.

They both stand, grab their trays and head for the exit. When we near the trash, Amy finally replies. "OK, I'm in."

Adam follows suit. "If you're set on doing this, I guess it wouldn't hurt to have a strong, muscular man with you." He smirks. "I still think this is dangerous and better left to the police," Adam continues while emptying his tray. "But I'm in."

"Great!" I exclaim. "Then let's get to work."

Chapter 30

"**W**ho wants Chinese?"

Chief Wright walks through the doors of the precinct carrying two white plastic bags filled with cartons of pork, chicken balls, rice, egg rolls, noodles and of course the most important part of any Chinese meal, fortune cookies. He plops the bags down in front of Stacy, letting the aroma surround her. She leans over, taking a long deep breath in.

"Mmmmm," She says after another long inhale. "Smells delicious!"

"I hope it is." Chief Wright replies. "It's going to be a long night. Let's set up in the conference room." Picking up the bags, he starts towards the back of the precinct before calling over his shoulder. "Do we still have those plates and forks?"

"I think so." Stacy answers. "I'll go check."

Locking her computer, she hurries over to the storage room, anxious to sink her teeth into some real food. Trail mix just isn't cutting it today. After rummaging through a few boxes, Stacy finds the remnants of Officer Randall's surprise birthday bash. Paper plates, plastic forks and cups, and even some party hats. Grabbing what she thinks will be enough, Stacy joins the others gathered in the conference room.

The paperwork, which had scattered the long table for days, has been pushed to one end. Chief Wright places the cartons at the other, bordered by cans of soda. Officers Randall and Martin drool while waiting to chow down. Stacy, after leaving the plates and forks with Chief Wright, takes the seat next to Officer Martin. As Stacy's hand slips below the table, a sheepish grin appears on his face.

"Three..." Chief Wright starts his usual countdown. "Two... One... Everybody dig in!" And they do. As always, the meat is the first thing to go.

"So, what do we know so far?" Chief Wright asks once everyone is settled.

"Well," Officer Randall sits straight up. "We've got stacks of both missing pets and missing persons." He motions to the reports at the end of the table. "Other than the locket and that canister, nothing has been found. There doesn't appear to be a motive. None of the victims have anything in common."

"I'm sure one person could shed some light." Chief Wright mumbles while stuffing the other half of his egg roll into his mouth.

"Are you still stuck on Ms. Crawford as our main suspect?" Officer Martin asks, trying to ignore the wandering hand on his thigh. "She's just a kid."

"A kid with a troubled past." Chief Wright replies. "This all started when she moved to town."

Officer Martin shakes his head. "The witnesses say spiders killed the victim and that Ms. Crawford fell into the room. If she did it, she wouldn't leave her bloody locket behind."

"What are you saying Martin?" Chief Wright bolts out of his seat.

"She's from the big city and you've never left Crescent Falls." Stacy's hand falls away as Officer Martin stands to face Chief Wright. "I think you're jealous, resentful and being an obsessive ass!"

"How dare you! You son of a b-"

The phone rings in the other room, freezing everyone and preventing an all-out war. Glares shoot across the table of empty cartons as the phone rings a second time. Stacy, wanting to escape the hostility that has permeated the room, rushes to her desk. She answers the phone mid ring.

"Is anybody gonna eat that?"

Officer Randall points towards the small amount of remaining rice. All he receives are cold stares. Swiping the tin tray, he dumps the remnants on his plate. Officer Randall feels the other men's eyes on him as he devours it. Two mouthfuls are all it takes. When he reaches for one of the fortune cookies, Stacy re-enters the room.

"Chief, I think you'll want to see this." She hands over a sheet of paper. "They said you wanted a rush put on it, so they bumped it to the top and faxed over the results."

Chief Wright relaxes as he reads over the document.

"What is it?" Officer Randall asks while cracking open his cookie. His lips curl down as he frowns at his fortune.

"The report on the canister we found." Chief Wright replies, returning to his seat. "Apparently the lab found traces of pheromones." He scans the page and reads off the key points. "Remote controlled device... Releases the pheromones into the air... One set of unidentified fingerprints."

"What does it mean Chief?" Officer Randall flicks his balled up fortune down the table.

Still fuming, but suddenly interested, Officer Martin answers, "What it means is that someone is controlling those spiders and using them to kill!"

"But who? If the fingerprints aren't in the system..." Officer Randall trails off.

Chief Wright locks eyes with Officer Martin. "I think it's time we brought Ms. Crawford in for questioning."

Chapter 31

The next day we set our plan into motion. Armed with a list of questions, we stop people before classes, between classes and during lunch. We come up dry. Other than a few missing pets, nobody has noticed anything. The fact that Nathan is still missing matters to no one.

I climb onto the bus at the end of the day, frustrated and disappointed. After finding an empty seat near the back, I watch as the other students deliberately pass the empty seat next to me. As the bus leaves the school behind, I focus on the world outside my window.

The bus comes to a stop a block from my house. Relieved to finally be home and away from these ignorant people, I grab my bag. While walking down the aisle, a foot darts out. Not today. I step over the outstretched leg and hurry off the bus.

A cool breeze caresses my face as I walk alone down the sidewalk. A couple passes on their bikes, waving. I wave back. A car speeds by as I approach my driveway. Through the strands of wind-blown hair covering my eyes, I can make out my mother sitting on the steps of the front porch.

"Hey Mom, what's up?" I drop my bag at the bottom of the steps and take a seat next to her.

"Chief Wright called." She places a hand on my knee. "He wants us to stop by the station as soon as possible. I think we should go now."

This doesn't really come as a shock. I figured he'd call eventually.

"Alright." I stand, grab my bag and head towards the car. "Let's get this over with."

The parking lot is packed when we arrive at the station. Somehow, my mother finds the one empty space and squeezes us in. The screaming reaches us before we can even enter the building. The small lobby is crowded with people, all directing their outbursts at the poor receptionist. An older woman is going on about her poor Poopsie while a man demands that someone find his missing dog.

The loudest of all though is the man at the front of the pack. The stains on his shirt are visible from my place near the entrance. I watch as he jiggles with every angry wave of his fist. The way he wheezes in between rants worries me. I feel he could collapse any minute.

"I've been here every day since he went missing! Nothing has been done!" He takes a deep breath. "You never called! When are you people going to get off your asses!" He slams his fist down on the desk. "I want answers NOW!"

The receptionist, to my surprise, doesn't even blink. She leans back in her chair, cool as can be and bats her long eyelashes. How I envy her restraint. If I was in her position he would have received a mouthful, if not a knock upside the head.

"Listen Timothy, I know you're upset. We are doing everything we can." The receptionist raises her well-manicured hands and motions to everyone else in the room. "As you can see though, we have other people that need our help as well."

"I don't care about anyone else!" Timothy appears ready to explode. "I WA-"

"ENOUGH!"

Everyone turns in unison as Chief Wright exits an office and slams the door behind him. The whole station has become quiet except for the faint ringing of a phone somewhere in back. My mother and I watch as he storms over to the main desk. With a stern look, he addresses the crowd.

"Those who have something to report, make a single file, QUIET line and Stacy here will talk to you one at a time. If you can't manage that," He points past us, making eye contact with me. "THERE'S THE DOOR!"

A few disgruntled people push past us, mumbling under their breath as they storm out. The rest obediently line up for their chance to speak with Stacy, the beautiful receptionist behind the desk.

"Ms. Crawford," Chief Wright continues to stare at me with those steely eyes. "You can follow me."

He leads us into a conference room at the back of the station. My mother and I sit on one side of a wooden table. Chief Wright, with his files, sits across from us. Bottles of water occupy the middle of the table, waiting to be snatched up. My mother and I both take one.

"First of all, I would like to thank you for coming in." Chief Wright opens a folder. "I appreciate the cooperation."

"Of course." My mother leans forward in her chair. "After what happened, we'll do anything to help."

"I'm glad you feel that way." He turns his attention to me. "Lily, I just have a few questions for you."

"Like my mom said, I'll do anything to help." I reply.

"Walk me through what happened at the theater. You were with Lucas McKinlay?" He asks, scanning over the papers in front of him. "Is that right?"

My mother silently sips her bottle of water, once again listening to me describe the horrible night.

"Yeah, I was with Luke. You know that. He went to use the washroom. After a bit, I could hear screaming. I got up to complain because I thought it was from one of the other movies. Then I saw Luke..." I shiver, remembering the scene. "We fell into the room. There was blood... on the walls... a puddle... on the floor."

"So that's when you lost your locket? When you fell?" The Chief stares at me, unblinking. "And you're sure that's the whole story?" I nod. "Didn't leave anything out?"

"Yeah, that's it. Why?" I respond, unsure of what he's referring to.

"Well, we found another piece of evidence with a set of fingerprints which are yet to be identified." He looks at my mother and then back at me. "Did you touch anything in that room? Would you be willing to let us fingerprint you?"

The wrinkles deepen across my mother's forehead. I try to think back. I remember the screams echoing through the lobby. Landing in the bathroom and seeing all the blood. Luke trying to get me out. Then it comes to me.

"I found something that looked like a silver can of spray paint, only smaller." I glance over at my mother and place my hand on hers. "It was behind the toilet. I don't know what I was thinking. Maybe I was just curious. Anyways, I picked it up. My fingerprints would probably be all over it."

"Great!" Chief Wright exclaims sarcastically, his nostrils flaring. "So you contaminated the crime scene... If what you say is true that is."

"Of course it's true." My mother suddenly leans over the table. "What reason would she have to lie? If she says she found it then that's what happened!"

The Chief leans back in his chair, arms crossed. I catch the words "likely story" as he mutters under his breath.

"WHAT WAS THAT?" My mother, leaping from her chair, goes ballistic. "WHAT DID YOU JUST SAY?"

"You're all the same. You think you can just come into our town, do whatever you want and get away with it." He stands to meet my mother's glare. "Well not this time!"

The door to the conference room bursts open. A clean shaven, short haired officer stands in the doorway, obviously concerned about the screaming.

"Officer Martin!" Chief Wright shouts. "Get Out!"

The officer fixes his gaze on the Chief and shakes his head with a look of disappointment.

"Come on Lily." My mother ushers me through the open door. "We're done here."

Chapter 32

"**B**randon let's go!"

Kate shouts up to her son from the main foyer, keys to the car in hand. If he had just gotten ready when Kate had told him, maybe Brandon wouldn't have missed the bus. As if dealing with the police last night wasn't enough, now she is going to be late for the staff meeting at the hospital. *Why can't he be more like Lily? Up early and out the door on time.*

"I'm coming, I'm coming." Brandon lumbers down the hall and looks at his mother from the top of the stairs. Zoey stands by his side, licking his hand. He descends at a snail's pace, Zoey following right behind.

"Grab your bag and get your shoes on." Kate tries hopelessly to fix his messy hair. "We've got to get a move on."

He slowly ties his shoes, picks up his waiting backpack and throws it over his shoulders. After saying goodbye to Zoey and giving her a large hug, Brandon drags his feet out the door. Kate locks up, rushes Brandon into the car and finally pulls out of the driveway.

Brandon's school is a small single-story building with an even smaller parking lot. Bike racks line the front of the building with gardens filling in the gaps. A chain-link fence surrounds the schoolyard which is host to a soccer field, baseball diamond and multiple portables. Basketball nets share the tarmac with hopscotch and foursquare courts. Just off the tarmac, there is of course a playground for the younger children, something Brandon wouldn't be caught dead on.

"Alright, off you go. I'll see you tonight." Kate barely comes to a stop in front of the school before Brandon swings the car door open and hops out. As he races towards the schoolyard Kate calls after him, "Don't miss your bus!"

On the tarmac, a group of girls sing. The hopping girl in the center does her best, but the skipping rope eventually hits her feet. Stepping over the now slack ropes, she notices Brandon passing and waves. His cheeks heat up and his pace increases.

"Hey Brandon, wait up!" Devon appears at his side. "Why is your face so red?"

"It's nothing." Brandon replies, taking a quick glance back.

Devon laughs. "You like Sarah."

"Shut up!" Brandon walks even faster, trying to distance himself from Sarah and her friends. "Don't tell anyone."

"OK buddy." Devon pats Brandon on the back. "Your secret is safe with me."

The bell rings as they arrive at the steps of the portable. They stand in line waiting for their teacher Mrs. Hall to show up. She exits the back of the school dressed in a black skirt that ends inches above her knees and a white blouse that is dangerously close to being transparent. Mr. Burk, the teacher's aide, walks beside her.

Once Mrs. Hall has unlocked the portable, Brandon and his classmates march single file into the classroom. The small space houses hooks at the rear for jackets, bags and other hangables, desks arranged in rows, and two aisles leading to a long blackboard. Mrs. Hall's desk sits at the front of the room next to one of the two windows.

Leaving his bag at the back, Brandon carries his books to his desk, which is next to Devon's of course. Opening his binder reveals sketches of hearts filled with the names Brandon and Sarah. He tries to cover it up before any prying eyes take notice. Too late. A smirk crosses Devon's face as he looks a row ahead and a few seats over in Sarah's direction.

Attendance is followed by Brandon's least favorite topic of all, math. Mr. Burk hands out a worksheet which the whole class works through together. Mrs. Hall calls on students to answer a few of the questions on the blackboard, encouraging them to show their work. Mr. Burk assists with any issues while Brandon does his best to avoid his teacher's gaze.

Question after question is answered until only one remains. Mrs. Hall's eyes fall upon Brandon. As her lips part, preparing to utter his name, the recess bell rings. The breath Brandon had been holding is released. Everyone closes their books, jumps out of their seats and rushes for the exit. Sarah holds the door and smiles at Brandon as he and Devon pass by. All Brandon can muster is, "Th...Thank you."

The Hill, a large grass covered mound, looms near the back of the schoolyard. During the winter months, The Hill is littered with students carrying sleds. Some however, prefer to slide down on their backs or even their feet, surfing their way to the bottom. Throughout the rest of the year, the trees sprouting from it provide plenty of shade.

"So when are you going to talk to her?" Devon asks, playfully elbowing Brandon. "She obviously likes you."

They take a seat under a large oak tree, watching the group of younger students below.

"You're it!" One of them squeals while slapping another on the back.

"I can't do that!" Brandon exclaims. "Everyone would make fun of me. It's hard enough just seeing her. I can't think straight when I do."

They spend the rest of recess talking about Sarah. Devon continues trying to convince Brandon to tell her how he feels. It fails.

They arrive at the portable to find it teacherless. Brandon, copying the other students, returns to his seat with Devon in tow. He watches the hands of the clock go round and round. Five minutes turns to ten before the door swings open.

"Since the sun is shining and it's not too cool yet, let's have gym outside. Before you know it, the snow will be falling." Mrs. Hall, as perky as ever, enters the room with Mr. Burk. She stops at her desk, opens a drawer and pulls out her whistle. "We are going to play a game we used to play when I was your age. Popcorn."

Hand after hand is raised. The same question is asked repeatedly. What is popcorn? The mystery reveals itself when they head outside and see the large parachute and a group of rubber balls. Mrs. Hall has everyone line up around the edge of the red and black parachute. Devon, always scheming, manages to get Brandon standing next to Sarah.

"So, to play popcorn, everyone will grab the edge of the parachute like this." Mrs. Hall bends over, revealing enough cleavage for Mr. Burk to drool over for weeks. "Then you will raise it up over your head." She lifts the edge up into the air. "And then bring it back down. Mr. Burk and I will throw some balls in and it will be like popcorn popping!" She drops the edge of the parachute to the ground without causing so much as a ripple across it. "Everyone ready?"

Brandon picks up the section of parachute before him, careful not to touch Sarah's hand in the process. Laughing and giggling fills the field as the students eagerly lift the parachute above their heads. Mr. Burk selects a couple rubber balls, preparing to toss them in. He watches the center pop up as the edges come down, releasing spots of red and black into the air. Eyes are raised as the specks fill the sky. Then the screaming begins.

Chapter 33

The parachute drifts to the ground as spiders descend on terrified victims. Mrs. Hall frantically runs her hands through her hair, knocking free those which have entangled themselves there. Another spider lands on her forehead before scurrying between the mounds on her chest.

Mr. Burk brushes a couple from his shirt while trying to round up the screaming children. One of the kids collapses next to the parachute. A red welt covers the better part of his short neck. Mr. Burk immediately rushes to the boy's side and shakes his unmoving body. No response.

Brandon and Devon, so far spider free, squash as many as they can. Sarah screams hysterically. Noticing movement on the back of her shirt, Brandon quickly swats the eight-legged creature away. He crushes it as it tries to escape through the grass.

"Everyone to the school!" Mrs. Hall shouts, tearing off her blouse. Multiple spiders fall to the ground. While eyes fixate on her lace bra, she points at the double doors, "NOW!" Mr. Burk picks up the unmoving child and ushers the other students towards safety. Heels clack on the tarmac as Mrs. Hall brings up the rear.

The doors shake as they slam against the inner walls. With everyone inside, Mrs. Hall drags a nearby table, art display included, towards the doors and uses it as a barricade. Nothing comes in and no one goes out.

Hearing all the commotion, the hallway begins to fill. Other teachers rush over, offering their assistance. The principal arrives, looks upon the unmoving child, and then hurries back towards the office.

"Here Hun." A plump woman hands Mrs. Hall a blue sweater. She pulls it over her head. It hangs off her skinny frame, but hides what it needs to.

"Is everyone here?" Mrs. Hall looks around the crowded hallway. Her eyes fall on Mr. Burk and the school nurse kneeling next to the child in his arms. "Is he OK?"

The reply she receives from the nurse is, "He's alive."

Examining the other children, Mrs. Hall takes note of red welts, numerous bites, and some slurred speech. A few students even report numbness in their arms and legs. She pats everyone down to ensure there are no more spiders hiding out. The wheels squeak as one of the teachers steers a metal cart loaded with juice boxes towards the group. Satisfied that the students are monster free, Mrs. Hall assists with handing them out.

The faint sound of sirens breaks through the chatter. They get louder and louder, eventually arriving in front of the school.

"Uh... what...happened?" The child in Mr. Burk's arms opens his eyes. "Where am I?"

Mrs. Hall drops an open juice box, allowing it to leak onto the floor. "Oh, thank God!" She places her hand over her heart and kneels down next to Mr. Burk. "It's OK. You're safe."

Paramedics burst through the doors. The principal meets and leads them over to Mr. Burk. After examining the child in his arms, the paramedics help Mr. Burk carry him out to the waiting ambulance.

Things are beginning to calm down when the doors fly open again. "What happened here?" Chief Wright asks, taking in the scene. "Somebody fill me in."

"It was just like on the news." Mrs. Hall says, taking the Chief aside. "Spiders, and lots of them." She details everything for the Chief, after which he pulls out his cell phone and presses a button.

"I'm at the elementary school." Chief Wright lowers his voice and whispers, "There's been another attack."

The paramedics return to check on the other children. They apply bandages to bites but don't find anything serious.

"Keep an eye on those that were bitten." One of the paramedics explains to Mrs. Hall. "Have their parents do the same. If anything should arise, bring them in immediately."

They leave and Mrs. Hall watches the ambulance pull away with Mr. Burk and the young boy riding in back.

When Chief Wright asks to see the scene, Mrs. Hall moves the table and leads him through the back doors. Cautious of any spiders, they make their way across the tarmac. The dark parachute lies unmoving. The ground around the parachute is littered with the bodies of squashed spiders. Chief Wright pulls a pen from his pocket and, bending down, pokes at one of the lifeless creatures.

"Chief!" Ed the exterminator calls from the rear doors of the school. "What the hell happened?"

"Language Ed!" Chief Wright shouts back. "Come over here."

Ed crosses the tarmac, a bag over his shoulder. Chief Wright recounts the events, pointing out all the bodies. Pulling on a pair of gloves, Ed picks one up and turns it over in his hands. He examines every nook and cranny before spending a good half hour inspecting the surrounding schoolyard. Nothing remains untouched by his prying eyes. Chief Wright and Mrs. Hall follow close-ly, pretending to understand all the technical jargon he spits out. After an extensive examination of the property they end up right back where they started.

"Well, there is no sign of a nest anywhere on the property and we didn't find any other spiders." Ed takes a jar from his pack and places one of the dead spiders in-side. "You know, I've never seen anything like these little ones. They certainly aren't from around here."

"So you're saying it's safe to go back to the class-room?" Mrs. Hall asks, anxious to put this behind her. "Parents are on the way. Can we let the students grab their things?"

"The coast is clear." Ed shakes the glass container, watching the lifeless body rattle around inside. "Let the children free."

While Chief Wright and Ed head out front to talk, Mrs. Hall rounds up her students. She leads the pack of nervous kids back across the tarmac to their portable. Everyone begins gathering their things.

"Ewww." Devon whispers, pointing at Brandon's shoes. "You've got one on you."

The lifeless body hangs off the side of Brandon's left shoelace. Trying to get rid of the creature, he swings his foot back and forth. When that fails, an idea comes to him. He finds an empty sandwich bag. Reaching down, Brandon pries away the dead spider which has become entangled in the threads of his shoelace. He places it in the bag, sealing it tight.

Chapter 34

It's been a week since the attack at my brother's school and the police still have nothing. My heart sank when I heard what happened. The attack at the theater was one thing, but now with my family as a possible target, this has become personal.

As for our investigation, Brandon may have inadvertently broken it wide open. He must have snuck into my room early this morning because when I awake, what do I see only a few inches from my face? A fuzzy spider. It isn't until my throat becomes hoarse from screaming that I realize it is already dead. That's also when I hear the laughter coming from the doorway. Brandon stands there, phone in hand, recording it all.

Flinging the pillow with the nightmarish intruder against the wall, I bound out of bed and chase Brandon all the way to the living room. Tackling him on the couch, I snatch the phone away. Zoey, appearing as if out of nowhere, decides to get in on things. She barks at us while I hold the phone out of Brandon's reach. Finding the file, I promptly delete it before I become the next viral video.

With my humiliating wakeup call wiped from existence, I stand and toss Brandon his phone. Before I allow him to escape though, I insist he tell me where the disgusting thing came from. The moment I hear that it came from his school, he loses my attention. I know spiders killed the man at the theater, but they were gone when I arrived. I have to get a good look at it.

After delivering one final punch to Brandon's shoulder, which elicits another loud bark from Zoey, I race to the kitchen where I find just what I need. My mother always packs her lunch with the dressing separate from her salad. Unfortunately, that won't be happening today. I return to my room with the round, plastic container.

The pillow still lies where I had flung it in my moment of terror. The spider however is nowhere in sight. I scour the carpeted floor in the surrounding vicinity but come up empty. It isn't until I begin moving furniture that I discover the dead carcass wedged between the back of my nightstand and the wall.

I scoop it up with the container and screw the lid on tight. Holding it close to my face, I peer through the transparent plastic at one of the creatures that have been causing so much havoc. It's about the size of a quarter and covered in short red and black hairs. Déjà vu strikes. I know I've seen one like this before but can't quite put my finger on where. The thought of delivering it to the police is quickly tossed. They probably have plenty more, and I would only be making Chief Wright's job easier if he found out I had one. Tucking it into my backpack, I decide to show Adam and Amy.

They arrive at my locker before first period, the look of anticipation filling their eyes. I guess the text I sent got their attention.

"So what's the news?" Amy asks, nearly jumping up and down. "What did you find?"

I explain this morning's excitement and present our new lead. Amy cringes. She takes a quick peek but refuses to get too close. Adam on the other hand takes the container and, holding it inches from his face, examines the carcass inside.

"So are you going to take it to the police?" Adam passes the container back, making an obvious point not to touch me. He crosses his arms and leans against the wall, his head resting next to an advertisement for the upcoming football game.

"They'd only use it as evidence against me." I carefully place the carcass into my backpack. "I figured we could do some research after school and see what we can find."

We make plans to meet in the library after school. When the warning bell rings, I ask Amy to go ahead so I can talk to Adam alone. Without question she turns and heads towards class, leaving us behind.

"What was that about?" I ask, lowering my voice. "I thought we were OK."

"I realize you're with... Luke" Adam spits the name out. "But can't we still pretend at school? It's not like he's going to find out."

We start making our way through the thinning heard of students.

"I said no, Adam." We stop just outside the classroom. "I don't want to do this anymore." A couple students pass between us. When Adam remains silent, I leave him alone in the hall.

The classroom is a buzz. The jocks are talking about tonight's practice and how they are going to crush the Eagles. The Snobettes stand at the front of the room, practicing for when they transform into cheerleaders. Settling in at my desk, I scan the rest of the class. It's about split. Half of the students look excited for the upcoming game while the other half couldn't seem to care less. Adam finally enters, quietly taking his seat. His father enters moments later, coffee in hand and appearing even more muscular than the week before, if that's possible.

After an otherwise uneventful day, we meet up in the library as planned. Not wanting to scare anyone with our little visitor, we select a couple computers as far out of sight as possible. I place the container between us as the web search begins. It doesn't take long for Amy to find an image that closely matches.

We gather around her computer as she clicks the associated link. It leads to a site with multiple images of what is labeled as the South American Social Spider. Amy continues to click on photos. One shows hundreds of these spiders building a web. Another is a close up displaying all the same markings as ours.

"South America?" Adam leans over Amy's shoulder, the silent treatment coming to an end. "How did they get here?"

"That's the big mystery." I say, eyes glued to the screen. "If we can find out how they got here, maybe we can figure out who's behind all this."

"And how are we supposed to do that?" Adam asks. "Do we even have any suspects?"

"Let's make a list." Amy spins in her chair and pulls a notebook and pen from her bag. Flipping to an empty page she writes People of Interest at the top. "OK, so what do we know so far?"

Chapter 35

"Jimmy!" Coach Olsen yells. "Get back on the field!"

Having infiltrated the cheerleader's small group, Jimmy's arms are wrapped around two of the most welcoming girls. Giggles abound as Jimmy holds one hand up to his helmet covered ear as if to say, "What was that?"

Following more shouts from the coach, Jimmy decides to return to practice. He makes a call me sign with his hands as he leaves the cheerleaders behind. The girls pick up their pom-poms. While jogging across the grass, Jimmy hears, "Go Cougars!"

"Keep it in your pants until after the game, Jim." Coach Olsen says when Jimmy rejoins the team. "The big game is tomorrow. Can you hold off that long?"

"Yes sir," Jimmy replies, the blood rushing to his face. He receives a few friendly slaps on the back. "I think I can manage."

"Well good. I'm glad to hear it." Coach Olsen tosses the football to Jimmy before addressing the team. "One lap. GO!"

The group begins circling the field while Coach Olsen prepares for the upcoming drills. Running turns to jogging turns to walking as the team approaches the cheerleader's practice. Mesmerized, the boys follow their legs up into the darkness of their very short skirts. Brittney, the head cheerleader, waves at the passing jocks before performing a front flip off the pyramid. Landing gracefully, she kneels and raises her pom-poms in the air.

Still drooling, the team finishes their lap. After a few passing and catching drills, Coach Olsen brings their attention to the five man tackling sled positioned on the field. The first row of five faces the sled. With their heads up, they charge. It gradually inches across the field. Coach Olsen stands on the back of the sled screaming, "Don't stop!"

After a short water break, Coach Olsen brings everyone together for a twenty minute scrimmage. Jimmy stands behind the center, the count is called and the ball is snapped. Having finished their practice, the cheerleaders gather at the sidelines to cheer them on.

With a score of 3-0, the scrimmage comes to an end. Helmets in hand, the team strides off the field.

"Good job out there guys." Coach Olsen passes around sports drinks. "Make sure to get some sleep. Tomorrow's going to be a big day." He chugs a bottle himself and then points towards the school. "Now hit the showers."

A couple cheerleaders remain, watching from the bleachers. Spotting them, Jimmy splits from his team. The showers can wait. As he approaches, the girls lean back and push out their chests. Grinning, he takes a seat between them, making a sandwich. Two slices of cheerleader with a quarterback filling.

"So girls, did you like what you saw?" Jimmy looks from one girl to the other. "I know I enjoyed watching you shake your... pom-poms."

"We loved every minute." One girl says, running a hand down Jimmy's muscular arm. "And we'd love to see more."

"Well then," Jimmy says, sporting a wide smile. "I'll give you my number and we can set up a private show."

Both girls eagerly pass their phones to Jimmy. He casually programs his number into each. Using their knees as support, Jimmy then stands and returns the phones. On his way towards the school, he looks back. "Don't forget to call!" He shouts. Both girls, oblivious to anything else, sit staring at their phones. Their eyes are wide with excitement.

The musty smell fills Jimmy's nostrils as he joins his team. With the showers running full blast, the whole locker room is warm and humid. After opening his locker, Jimmy strips down, grabs a towel and hits the showers.

The water is running but no one's home. Circling the empty space, he turns off all but one. Enjoying his time alone, Jimmy relaxes within the steamy mist.

Realizing he can't stay forever, Jimmy eventually returns to his locker, clean and towel covered. Reaching into his locker, he collects his clothes. The moment his boxers are on, Jimmy feels the sting of a spun towel across his cheeks. Instinctively grabbing his rear, he spins around to face his assailant and their accompanying laughter.

"Keep it in your pants Jim." Daniel, the team's center and Jimmy's best friend, mocks Coach Olsen. He spins the wet towel, preparing for another attack. "Do you think you can manage that?"

The towel misses its target as Jimmy dodges. Before Daniel can try again, Jimmy grabs and tugs the towel from his hand. He spins it and quickly returns fire. The weapon meets its mark, leaving a red welt on Daniel's upper thigh.

"OK," Daniel says, holding up his arms. "Truce. You win."

"Damn right I win." Jimmy drops the wet towel with a grin and returns to getting dressed.

"So are you going to the party tomorrow?" Daniel pulls on his shirt. "It's supposed to be pretty big."

"Oh, I'll be there." Jimmy pulls on a pair of jeans.

The rest of the team, now dressed, begins to clear out. Daniel stuffs his uniform into a gym bag and shuts his locker. Sitting topless on a bench, Jimmy slips on a pair of socks and shoes. Placing his hand on Jimmy's back, Daniel says goodnight and leaves him alone in the room. Last one out again.

Standing, Jimmy pulls his shirt over his head and closes his locker. Just as metal meets metal, the lights in the room go out. Other than the sliver of late afternoon sun seeping in from the storage room window, it is pitch black.

"Who's there?" Jimmy feels his way along the lockers, inching towards the change room door and the switch.

When his eyes begin adjusting to the darkness, Jimmy moves faster. He rounds the corner of the lockers and notices something coming quickly towards him. Ducking, the aluminum bat skims over his head and smashes loudly against the metal lockers. Standing before him, Jimmy can make out someone dressed all in black. In their hands is one of the bats from the storage room and strapped to their head is a pair of high tech looking goggles.

Dropping quickly, Jimmy swings his legs out before the dark figure has a chance to react. They stumble backwards and land on the floor, hitting the back of their head in the process. Crawling forward, Jimmy climbs on top of the dark figure. He reaches for the goggles and mask covering their face.

Jimmy's body becomes rigid as the volts flow through him. The dark figure forcefully presses the Taser against Jimmy's ribs. With one good shove, the dark figure rolls him off. Lying on his back, Jimmy holds his side. He watches in terror as the dark figure stands and picks up the bat.

Chapter 36

Before he opens his eyes, Jimmy feels the warm trickle of blood along the side of his face. It reaches his jaw, slows, and then continues down the side of his neck. The next thing to come is the faint sound of dripping over head. Drip. Drip. Drip. Blinking, Jimmy finally opens his eyes.

The lights are back on. Trying to stand, his head smacks against the porcelain sink above. That's when he realizes his hands are bound and tied to a pipe. Looking down, he observes the rope that also binds his legs. Panicking, he tries to call for help. His screams are muffled by the rag in his mouth and the tape securing it.

Frantically scanning the room for some way of escaping, his eyes fall upon his worst nightmare. Standing in the far corner, the dark figure watches in silence while using the now bloody bat as a cane. Jimmy stares wide eyed as the dark figure simply raises a gloved hand and waves.

Jimmy begins to struggle. Using his bound hands, he tugs with all his might on the pipe holding him in place. It starts to give as the dark figure moves forward. Standing in front of Jimmy, the dark figure reaches inside their black jacket and pulls out a silver spray can. Nozzle pointed at Jimmy, they spray him directly in the face and then continue to coat his whole body. With the deed complete, the dark figure once again retreats to their corner.

One last tug and the pipe breaks. Water gushes forth as Jimmy frees his hands. It pours over his head and cascades down his back. Pinching an edge of the tape between his fingers, Jimmy peels it from his mouth and promptly spits out the dirty rag. Using his teeth, he pulls on the knot binding his hands until the rope falls away.

"Who the FUCK are you?" Jimmy reaches down to untie his legs. "What do you want?"

The dark figure points in the direction of the storage room. Following the pointed finger, Jimmy spots the first spider emerge from the doorway. His pulse quickens as an unending line of spiders heads his way.

"HELP ME!" Fingers move quickly, but the knot is too tight. Jimmy yanks on the rope. "DO SOMETHING!"

The dark figure slowly shakes their head in response to Jimmy's pleas. Pushing himself up, Jimmy begins hopping to the door with his legs still bound. On the second hop, he slips in the growing pool of water. His nose slams against the tile floor. The surrounding water turns a reddish color as the blood flows. Not one to give up, Jimmy tries again. Back on his feet, he leaves a trail of blood spots as he hops towards the exit.

He is halfway to the door when the first spider reaches his sneakers. Jumping in place, Jimmy tries crushing the swarm beneath his feet. He is doing well at first, but they keep coming. Eventually there are too many and they overtake Jimmy, crawling up the inside of his pant legs.

His screams fall on deaf ears as the spiders sink their fangs into the flesh of both his legs. The paralysis begins to set in and Jimmy lowers himself back to the floor. Screams turn to whimpers as he maneuvers himself into a sitting position against the wall. Jimmy watches as spider after spider skims across the surface of the rose tinted pool.

The jeans covering his legs rise and fall as the spiders continue to crawl inside. Tears mix with blood as he comes to accept his fate.

"Why?" Jimmy's voice cracks as he looks at the dark figure. "Why would you do this?"

Receiving nothing other than a steely glare, Jimmy returns his attention to his legs. His left pant leg gently rises, then falls, rises again and then partially drops to the floor. The length of flattened pant leg increases as he watches his foot move further and further away. The screaming begins again. Streaks of blood mark the floor as the leg is dragged into full view. Jimmy nearly faints when he sees the jagged tears of flesh and muscle. The heads of his tibia and fibula slightly poke out of the mangled flesh.

When the spiders begin spinning his leg, Jimmy closes his eyes tight and prays for a miracle. The sudden sound of aluminum hitting tile jolts his eyes open. The dark figure stands in the corner shaking their head as if saying, "Don't you dare close them again." Jimmy spots a web sack being dragged towards the storage room. Noticing the tip of his sneaker sticking through the silk causes him to empty his stomach all over the floor.

Returning moments later, the spiders scurry through the chunks that used to be his lunch and make their way up his right pant leg. Once again, his pant leg rises and falls. When he tries to swat them away, Jimmy feels a growing tingling sensation in his fingers. Taking a deep breath he lets forth one long scream.

"Jimmy? Is that you?" Daniel calls from the other side of the door. He tries to push his way in but the door doesn't budge. "Why is the door locked?"

"Danny, HELP!" Imbued with hope, Jimmy uses his upper body to shake off as many spiders as possible. "HURRY!"

The door creaks as Daniel slams all his weight against it. While Jimmy continues to shake himself he quickly scans the room. The dark figure has vanished. Determined to survive, Jimmy leaves his sitting position and falls to his side. Fighting through the lightheadedness, he rolls himself over, crushing numerous spiders in the process. He does it again and again as multiple voices arrive on the other side of the door.

"OK, on the count of three," Daniel says. "One... Two... Three!"

Chapter 37

The sirens reach the library where I sit alone, continuing to research the South American Social Spider. An hour has passed since Adam and Amy left. Apparently dinner is more important. At least we spent a good thirty minutes working on our list of suspects before they abandoned me. Of course both had insisted that Jimmy and each one of the Snobettes be included. A few of the teachers were added as well. With the attacks being so random though, it could be anyone.

What sounds like a stampede passes the library. Could it be? I jump out of my seat, toppling it over in the process. After stuffing everything back into my bag, I rush past the librarian as she prepares to close for the day.

The hallway is deserted, but I can hear a lot of commotion coming from the direction of the gymnasium. Intent on finding out what has happened, I sprint down the hall, turn the corner and run into Amy. Knocking each other off balance, we both end up on the floor. The book Amy was carrying slides across the floor.

"What are you doing here?" With a literal pain in my ass, I stand and then help Amy to her feet. "I thought you went home."

"I was on my way when I realized I forgot my science book." Reaching down, Amy retrieves it. "I was just about to leave when I heard the sirens. What happened?"

"I don't know." I say, already walking away. "Let's find out."

Changing into reporter mode, Amy stashes the textbook in her bag and replaces it with a pocket sized notebook and pen. We make our way down the eerie hallway together. Why do buildings turn creepy after hours?

"Out of the way!" Two paramedics race towards us pushing a stretcher. We leap to the side as they breeze past, nearly clipping us. The wheels of the stretcher squeak as they turn the next corner. The hairs on the back of my neck rise as a terrible scream echoes through the hall.

"That sounds like Jimmy." Amy says, more to herself than me.

When we reach the gym, we realize just how serious things are. Chief Wright works with the goateed officer to keep what appears to be the entire football team plus a couple cheerleaders from reaching the boy's locker room. Screams continue to erupt from behind the closed door. Daniel, one of Jimmy's jock buddies, stands away from the group, talking with another officer. Tears streak his face as he explains what happened.

"I heard Jimmy... screaming for... help," Daniel says in between sniffles. "I tried to open the door... It was locked... I couldn't get it open... I called some of the other guys... It was too late... If I was stronger... then maybe..."

Daniel starts bawling. The officer tries to console him, unsuccessfully. Daniel slides down the wall, sits on the floor and buries his face in his hands. What did he mean? Is Jimmy alive? While trying to stay as far out of sight as possible, I watch as he visibly convulses with each sob. Seeing a tough guy like Daniel display that much emotion strikes a chord and my eyes start to water as well. I look at Amy standing next to me, scribbling furiously in her notebook. Her pen flies over the page. She doesn't appear to be phased by the current situation at all, which I guess is a good quality for a reporter.

When the door to the locker room opens, everyone pushes a little closer. The howls magnify. Amy and I try to sneak closer as well but are spotted by Chief Wright. He looks directly at me and says nothing, instead leaving me alone for once. The other students however, glare as if to say, "What the hell do you think you're doing here?"

One of the paramedics exits the locker room and, with the assistance of an officer, clears a path through the on lookers. The other paramedic then begins pushing the stretcher through the open door. Jimmy lies on the stretcher, sheet covered. His friends' calls are returned with screams of gibberish. I manage to make out some of the words. Person in black, spiders, my leg.

I start to wonder what he means about his leg but it doesn't take long to find out. As the stretcher passes through the locker room door, the sheet gets caught. Before anyone realizes what is happening, the sheet falls to the floor. One of the cheerleaders faints into the arms of the guy behind her while the others cry out in shock. We all get a perfect view of the blood soaked bandages covering the remnants of Jimmy's left leg. My stomach turns.

Quickly grabbing the sheet, the paramedics throw it back over Jimmy. They wheel him past the group of students and hurry down the hall towards the waiting ambulance. The crowd pushes past us, nearly knocking us to the floor as they chase after Jimmy and his wails. Chief Wright turns his attention to Daniel who continues to sob on the floor. He convinces Daniel to stand and then walks him out. The remaining officers enter the locker room, leaving Amy and I standing alone.

"I guess we can cross him off the list." Amy looks up from her notes. An unsettling grin crosses her face. "Looks like he finally got what he deserved."

Chapter 38

The school was going to cancel the football game until the team protested, insisting on playing and dedicating it to Jimmy. I had assumed school would be closed, but the game must be important to the police department as well. They finished their work and had the boy's locker room open by lunchtime.

Amy, apparently unable to trust the other student reporters to cover a sporting event, insisted on being at the game. Of course, not wanting to go alone, she drags me along. It's a hike, but when we arrive I'm glad we walked. The lot is packed. Groups of students, wearing blue and yellow jerseys, push their way towards the field behind the school. Others carry miniature flags with an image of a cougar surrounded by the same colors. A bus, with the name Eagles painted on the side, sits at the edge of the lot. Obviously the other team's transportation. As Amy and I proceed through the crowd, we pass a pick-up with the tailgate down. Cases of beer and numerous students surround it. That won't last long.

The stadium is overflowing with what could easily be the whole town. I'm shocked to see so many people. I didn't realize how big high school football really was. A group of young guys, their faces painted with the team colors, hold a banner with the words GO COUGARS!

Amy continues making notes as we head into the swarm of people. We come across a man next to the bleachers selling hotdogs and hamburgers. Demanding I experience everything, Amy pulls me into the long line. After a good ten minutes we finally reach the front. I order a bottle of water and a hotdog which the man pries off the grill, places on a crusty bun and hands to me on a paper plate. After handing over five bucks, I step aside and wait for Amy to order hers.

In the bleachers, we find a couple of empty seats between an elderly couple and another group of young guys. I sit, paper plate in my lap. As I bite into the bun it crunches and falls apart. Amy appears to be enjoying her burger and two hotdogs. She licks her lips and sinks her teeth into her burger. The grease runs down her chin as she then proceeds to chug a large soda. Man that girl can eat.

The music starts and the crowd rises, breaking into cheers and shouts. The elderly couple next to me is surprisingly some of the loudest. They shout and holler to our school's mascot running across the field. I have to stand in order to see over everyone else. Amy joins me, pen and paper back in hand.

The other team's mascot, an eagle, skips across the field while the other half of the bleaches breaks into cheers. Both mascots meet at the fifty-yard line where they look each other up and down. When it appears that a fight might break out, our mascot starts dancing. This is accompanied by more cheering from the stands. Our mascot finishes and then points at the eagle, turning it into a dance off. They take turns matching each other's moves before adding a little more. Eventually they are both breakdancing, complete with head spins, jackhammers and windmills.

When it becomes obvious that the cougar is unbeatable, the eagle hangs his head in shame. As our mascot gloats and raises his arms in the air, the eagle jokingly slaps him with a wing and skips away. The cougar shakes his head and races after him. Catching up, he pounces and wrestles the eagle to the ground. Sitting on his prey, he holds his hands together and shakes them above his head in victory. The bleachers erupt in applause. I surprise myself by joining in.

As the music changes, the mascots chase each other off the field. A large inflatable cougar head rolls towards the nearest end zone. Speakers crackle and then an announcer introduces us to the Crescent Falls Cougars. The banner concealing the mouth of the cougar splits open as the team jogs through. They wave to the audience as the head, which I can now see has a tunnel running through the center, stops at the edge of the field. When the team reaches their bench, Daniel is passed a microphone. He walks to the center of the field where he gives a touching speech regarding Jimmy. He nearly brings me to tears when he concludes with, "This game's for you, buddy."

It's about twenty minutes in and we are leading with a score of 9-7. My eyes are glued to the game when Amy stands.

"I shouldn't have had all that soda. I'll be right back." As Amy worms her way through the crowd, she calls back, "Wouldn't want to miss the half time show."

It seems like she is gone forever. Amy misses a touchdown by Daniel and a play which the older gentleman next to me enjoys so much that his dentures fly out of his mouth. They bounce off the head of the person in front of him before landing at his feet. When he brushes them off and places them back in his mouth, the elderly woman next to him scrunches her nose. "Harold, that's disgusting."

"Come now, Gladys." He replies, adjusting his teeth. "I've seen you do worse."

There's a solid hit by the other team. The man behind me obviously wasn't prepared. When everyone jumps out of their seats, he quickly follows suit, dropping his hotdog. I feel it slide slowly down the back of my shirt, ketchup and mustard smearing in. Amy would have got a kick out of that.

The whistle blows for half time and, as if on cue, Amy appears with a tray of nachos. When she sits, I reach over and grab a handful. A nacho crunches between my teeth as the cheering begins again.

"Looks like the show's about to start." Pulling out her notebook, Amy flips to a new page.

The school band marches into view. The sound of trumpets, tubas and drums fill the air as the cheerleaders flip towards center field. The band separates and circles the cheerleaders while they perform their routine. As mean as those girls can be, they sure have some moves. Continuing to play, the band positions themselves half on one side of the cheerleaders, half on the other. Flips and tumbles abound. As the routine nears its end, the cheerleaders build a human pyramid with Brittney on top. The music stops and Brittney is tossed into the air for the finale.

A loud bang, followed by seven more, breaks the silence. The bleachers shake as the audience jumps in unison. The band looks around, obviously confused at this unexpected event. Confetti begins to flutter down over the field. Someone yells, "Spiders!" This is when I realize there is more than confetti falling from the sky. I watch as the pyramid dissolves. My hand covers my mouth as Brittney, still in the air, loses focus in the middle of her flip. She proceeds to fall head first towards the ground. With no one there to catch her, she gets closer and closer. A blue piece of confetti lands on my hand as the crack echoes through the stadium.

Chapter 39

"**B**rittney!"

A woman, whom I assume is Brittney's mother, screams out as she watches her hit the ground. The other cheerleaders, while swatting at their legs, gather around Brittney. Her head is bent to the side. She doesn't appear to be moving. One of them grabs her shoulders and shakes, causing her head to roll back and forth.

The tuba player slams his instrument against the confetti covered ground, squashing the spiders crawling towards him. One of the drummers collapses, his leg coated in red and black. Dropping their instruments, other band members rush to his side. They brush spiders away while working together to drag him from harm's way. Players from both teams storm the field, stomping on anything that moves. Daniel arrives at Brittney's side and without hesitation, lifts her up and carries her past the end zone. Her parents meet Daniel. They plead for Brittney to wake up.

With all the excitement on the field, I have been too distracted to notice the commotion around me. People shove past each other, trying to reach the edge of the bleachers. A group of men charges past, oblivious to anyone else, and clips Harold. They continue to strong arm their way through the shrieking crowd as Harold loses his balance and falls backwards into Gladys. Before I can reach out, they both topple like a pair of dominoes. Harold's head connects with Gladys' face. She cries out, spraying the railing with blood. I bend down to help them when someone hits me from behind. Tripping over the couple, I let out a cry of my own as my forehead strikes the edge of a bench. Another scream escapes me when someone crushes my hand beneath their feet.

"Lily, are you OK?" Amy comes to my aide. When she gets a look at my face, she freezes. "You're bleeding pretty bad." She says. "We should get you to a doctor."

Feeling faint, I lean against the railing while Amy helps the elderly couple. Then, with my non-throbbing hand, I hold Amy's arm as she leads me off the bleachers. The elderly couple sticks closely behind.

I hear sirens as we pass the barbeque which now lies on its side. Burger patties, hot dogs, nachos and buns litter the ground. I spot a crowd gathered behind the bleachers. Brittney is on the ground, her mother and father kneeling at her side. Both parents weep while Daniel performs CPR. Brittney's chest rises and falls as Daniel breathes into her before returning to compressions. The dark bruise across her neck is nearly overshadowed by the red welts covering her legs.

Amy, her hand on mine, pulls me towards the parking lot. An ambulance pulls in, directly followed by another. Then the honking starts. Everyone attempting to leave at once has created a large traffic jam. The ambulance drivers continue to blare their horns as they force their way through.

When the first ambulance reaches the end of the parking lot, the two paramedics from yesterday jump out. They sprint towards Brittney as a van and two squad cars screech to a halt. Having no choice, they park on the road.

Chief Wright is in deep conversation with Ed when he passes us. He acknowledges me with a look and a nod. I watch as they join up with Principal Harris. The other officers construct a barrier, stopping anyone else from leaving. They begin taking statements.

A loud wail surprises both Amy and I. We spin around. One of the paramedics rises from his place beside Brittney and shakes his head. The other paramedic slowly returns to the ambulance, his eyes lowered. Brittney's mother lets out another loud wail as she covers her face with her hands. Her husband falls to his knees behind her and pulls her close. The other cheerleaders begin to sob in the arms of the nearby football players. The paramedic returns with a stretcher. Brittney is lifted onto it, covered with a sheet and rolled towards the ambulance.

Movement catches my eye. I spot Chief Wright on the field with Ed the exterminator. He examines the grass before drawing Ed's attention to different areas along the bleachers. He points at what appear to be small cannons.

The second ambulance finally breaks free from the sea of vehicles and parks next to the first.

"Let's get you checked out." Amy says. With an injured hand and a face streaked with both fresh and dried blood, I follow her lead.

Another set of paramedics appear. A young man and woman. After directing me to take a seat in the back of the ambulance, they examine me.

"You're definitely going to need stitches." The man says as he wraps a bandage around my forehead.

The young woman presses firmly on my hand. Pain shoots up my arm. "Well, it's going to hurt for a while," she says. "But nothing seems broken. Let's get you to the hospital."

Amy joins me before the paramedics shut the doors. They step into the front of the ambulance and we begin to move. As we pull onto the road, Amy turns to me. She tries to stifle her laughter. "I guess we can cross the Snobettes off the list too."

Chapter 40

"**A**re you comfortable Hun? Do you need some more pillows?"

"I'm fine Mom," Jimmy replies to his mother's babying.

Following the attack, Jimmy was rushed into surgery. Avoiding infection and closing the wound had been top priority. He had lost a lot of blood. The surgery was touch and go for a while, but he pulled through. The rest of the night was spent in recovery. His parents never left his side. This morning he was transferred to a private room where he was hooked up to an IV. When a doctor visited to discuss prosthetics, Jimmy would hear none of it. His screaming had chased the doctor from the room.

With all the drugs flowing through him, Jimmy no longer feels the pain of his injuries. Lying in his hospital bed, all he feels is numb. And anger. A growing anger at the world and the person responsible for taking his leg. When Jimmy is finally ready to leave the hospital, he vows to make that person pay.

"How about some water?" Jimmy's mother continues. "Or another blanket?"

"He said he was fine." Jimmy's father rises from his chair in the corner and places his hand on his wife's. "It'll be OK."

"I know, I know," She says, looking into his eyes. "I just have to do something. I feel so... helpless."

After filling a cup with water and placing it on the table next to Jimmy, she reluctantly steps away from his bed. She collects a couple tissues, retires to her husband's side and dabs at her eyes.

"You know, it's getting late and I'm kind of tired." Jimmy raises his hand to his mouth and fakes a yawn. "Why don't you guys head home and get some sleep."

"We don't want to leave you." Jimmy's mother balls up the tissue in her hand. "We can just sleep here again."

"I'll be fine. Probably just watch some TV and fall asleep," Jimmy replies, picking up the remote for the television.

"We can stay and watch with-"

"I WANT TO BE ALONE!" Jimmy bursts, cutting his mother off.

Shocked, both parents stand in silence. Jimmy's mother stares, her mouth slightly agape. She starts to reply but stops herself. She walks over to Jimmy and kisses his cheek. Her hand rests briefly on Jimmy's before she turns and walks out of the room without looking back.

Jimmy's father approaches the bedside. "We'll see you tomorrow." Jimmy turns his head away in shame, focusing on the window and the darkness beyond. "We love you Son."

When his father leaves, Jimmy turns and glances at the closed door. "I love you too," he whispers.

In an effort to distract himself from his thoughts and the unsettling silence of the empty room, Jimmy turns on the television. An old western fills the screen. Flipping through the other channels reveals nothing but static. Returning to the western, Jimmy watches with heavy eyes as a shoot-out begins. His eyes grow heavier and heavier as the bullets continue to fly. The squeak of sneakers filling the hallway isn't enough to keep him awake. He falls asleep as multiple people race past his room. The movie continues to play.

He wakes up shivering. Jimmy lifts his head from the pillow and groggily looks around the room. The only light comes from the glow of the television with the rolling credits. Jimmy pulls the sheets closer as a cool breeze blows through the wide open window.

He listens for movement in the hall. Nothing. The sudden sound of scraping reaches him. Metal on metal. Jimmy covers his ears and stares into the darkness under the corner television. The scraping continues as Jimmy's eyes try to adjust. Then, as quick as it began, the noise stops. Jimmy watches in horror as the dark figure steps out of the shadows and into the glow of the television screen.

Jimmy immediately reaches for the call button next to his bed. It goes slack in his hand. Pulling the attached cord, he realizes it has been cut. The dark figure holds up the knife in their right hand. The call button hits the floor. Jimmy screams for help. Nobody comes. He continues, but his screams go unanswered. Giving up hope, Jimmy turns his attention back to the dark figure in the corner.

"What do you want?" Jimmy, now more angry than frightened, sits up in the bed. "Wasn't taking my leg enough?"

The dark figure silently responds with a simple shake of the head.

"Then what do you want?"

Again the dark figure doesn't speak. They raise their left hand and point directly at Jimmy. With their right, they bring the knife up and lightly drag it across their throat.

Chapter 41

The nurse sits across from me, her skinny frame barely covering her seat. If a strong wind blew past, I bet she would snap in half. Her pen glides across the paper in front of her as she asks me question after question. When did it happen? How did it happen? Do I have any allergies?

The door to the exam room bursts open and we both jump. The pen slips from the nurse's hand and rolls to a stop beneath her chair.

"Lily? What ha..." My mother pauses in the doorway like a deer caught in a set of headlights. "Oh my god!"

The nurse steps back as my mother races to my side. She slowly removes the blood-soaked bandage from my forehead and inhales sharply.

"I was at the game with Amy when... Ouch!" I cry out, wincing in pain as my mother examines the cut.

"Is Amy here? I didn't see her out front." She continues to press around the wound while I clench my teeth and bare it. "You're definitely going to need a few stitches."

The twig-like nurse takes this as her queue and begins gathering items from the nearby drawers. She lays them on the counter and then places a cloth covered tray on a steel table with wheels. My mother washes her hands while the nurse rolls the table next to me and removes the cloth covering from the tray. She then opens a pack of gloves and holds the package, arms extended. My mother takes the gloves and dons them. The nurse then begins opening packages and dropping items onto the tray. When I see the needle, my eyes go wide.

"Is this going to hurt?" I try to prepare myself for the pain.

"I'm going to give you something to numb the area, but the needle might sting a little." My mother dips a swab in some liquid from a steel cup and cleans the area around the gash in my forehead. She then picks up the needle as the nurse holds a vial of what I assume is the stuff to freeze my forehead. The nurse says the name of the drug and my mother draws some into the syringe. I close my eyes and grip the edge of my seat.

I feel a slight pinch and then it's over. Opening my eyes, I watch my mother toss the needle into a plastic container. She then uses what looks like a pair of pliers to pick up a tiny needle and thread. I guess those are the stitches.

"How are you doing, Honey?" My mother pokes at my forehead with the needle but I feel nothing. "Ready for me to continue?"

"Yeah, let's just get this over with."

The whole process is quick and painless. Before I know it my mother is done. While she places a bandage over my stitches, the nurse cleans up. Once the room is back to the way it began, my mother and I are left alone in the exam room.

"So Mom, how did you know I was here?" I ask.

"I got called in." My mother seats herself across from me. "They told me there was an accident at the football game and a lot of people were hurt." She takes my sore hand in hers. "I raced in, leaving your brother with Mary. When I got here I saw your name on the list of patients." She bends one of my fingers and I pull my hand away. "Well, your hand seems fine." She looks into my eyes. "So what happened exactly?"

"Confetti cannons went off during the half time show. Brittney died." I cringe, remembering the loud crack. "There were spiders everywhere. Someone ran into me and I fell."

"Spiders? Your classmate that was attacked mentioned them as well."

"That's right! Jimmy's here. Maybe I should go visit him." My investigative instincts kick in. I might be able to get some details from him.

"Well, if you're feeling up to it I'm sure he'd enjoy company. Maybe you can mend some bridges." Her expression turns serious. "But no fighting. I mean it Lily. And come find me when you're done. I don't want you being alone."

My mother lets me know where his room is before leaving to meet the next patient on her list. I head back to the waiting room. Any hopes I had of bringing Amy with me quickly fade. The room is as crowded and loud as before only now an elderly man occupies Amy's seat. She probably just went for coffee. I decide to visit Jimmy alone.

It feels like I'm on the set of a horror movie as I make my way through the twisting hallways. I hear dripping somewhere in the distance, a couple of the lights are flickering and I haven't passed another soul yet. It must be all hands on deck in the ER.

I'm almost to Jimmy's room when an alarm starts blaring and a muffled voice comes through the speakers. It mumbles something followed by Jimmy's room number. I run down the hall, my shoes squeaking on the floor. I turn the corner to find a group of people already swarming Jimmy's door. They see me coming and try to hold me back. I push my way through.

Beyond the open door I view all that is left of Jimmy. His severed head sits atop a blood stained pillow. The expression of horror still frozen on his face. The sheets are soaked with red. It drips from the bed, forming a small puddle beneath. The rest of his body is nowhere in sight, although I imagine it was taken through the open window on the other side of the room.

Unable to hold back anymore, I drop to my knees and cover the linoleum floor with my dinner. While keeled over and retching, I notice a slight glimmer coming from under the mattress. Something in me says to take a closer look. I crawl towards the dripping sheets, avoiding the red puddles and ignoring the people trying to stop me. I reach under the bed and pull out my silver locket.

Chapter 42

I toss and turn at night, unable to sleep. I still see Jimmy's face staring back at me. Who would do such a thing? And why was my locket there? Certainly Jimmy didn't have it.

"Everybody off." The bus driver pulls to a stop in front of the school.

Following a week long closure, class is back in session. Everyone begins to pile off the bus, gawking at me as they pass. They call me names under their breath and laugh amongst themselves. The scar across my forehead has earned me multiple nicknames. Many make reference to a famous mobster movie but my favorites so far are Monster and The Creation. All I need now are a couple bolts in my neck and the transformation will be complete. At least it happened just in time for Halloween.

As I climb off the bus behind my giggling classmates, the bus driver closes the door, nearly catching my backpack. He starts to pull away when a few students scurry past the front of the bus. The driver leans on the horn.

Approaching the main doors, I realize how eager the school is to switch focus away from the accident and lighten the mood. Two lively skeletons, taped to the inside of the doors, tip their hats to me as I enter. Pumpkin cutouts and fake cobwebs line the walls. Witches on brooms and eerie ghosts hang from the ceiling. Whoever was in charge of decorations must have enjoyed themselves.

Amy and Adam are already in class when I arrive and take my seat. The remaining Snobettes sit quietly at the side of the room. Brittney's desk sits empty before them. It may be horrible, but at least the nastiness has calmed down. For the time being anyway.

Mrs. Davis appears once again as a substitute for Mr. Walker. She places her things on the desk and prints her name on the blackboard.

"Where's your dad?" I turn to Adam as Mrs. Davis hands around the day's assignment. "Is he sick?"

"Yeah, he spends most of his time in his room. I think it's the flu or something." Adam replies before adding, "Tis the season."

"Well, give him our best. I hope he gets well soon." I reply before changing the subject. "So any more news on you know what?"

Suddenly alert and beaming with excitement, Amy chimes in, "I've got some. How about we get together at lunch?"

After my morning classes, I wait for them behind the school. Amy arrives first. Adam, dragging his heels, shows up ten minutes later. With the gang together, I lead the way towards the empty bleachers. The area is quiet which is perfect for our meeting. Most people are avoiding this place like the plague. I honestly don't blame them.

Amy pulls her notebook from her bag and flips through page after page. Adam and I sit there like little children waiting for story time. She finally finds what she was looking for and turns to us.

"So far I haven't uncovered any more information regarding South America." Adam looks as disappointed as I feel upon hearing this. "But," Amy continues. "I visited the police station last week to talk to someone, anyone, about what happened at the game. I wanted to get what I could for the paper. At first nobody would speak to me." Amy smiles and then looks down at her notes. "I finally found someone who was more than willing to share."

I feel a shiver run through me and visibly shake. Adam notices and tries to comfort me. I casually brush him off.

Amy shoots me a questioning look before proceeding. "They told me that the confetti cannons were remote controlled and that the controller was missing."

"So someone set them off remotely?" I feel the adrenalin start pumping and lean even closer.

"Exactly! And here's the best part." Amy pauses as if trying to build the suspense. "They found traces of pheromones and believe someone is using them to control the spiders."

"Holy shit!" Adam looks stunned. "So there is someone out there controlling these spiders? Making them kill?"

"It certainly looks that way." Amy closes her notebook and tucks it back in her bag.

"Wow..." Is all I manage to say. I think about Brandon and wonder why anyone would attack his school.

"So are you going to print this?" Adam asks. "People should know."

"I don't think so. It would be a great story but I don't want to get my source in trouble." Amy replies. "They asked me to keep it between us."

"Who cares about your s-"

"I found my locket." It spills out of me, cutting Adam off. The details of Jimmy's death have yet to be released. All the public knows is that he passed away while in the hospital. I pull the locket from my pocket. The silver glistens in the sunlight.

"What?" Amy exclaims. "Where?"

I fill them both in on how I came to be back in possession of my locket. I detail every last gruesome moment. The severed head. The pools of blood.

"How could Jimmy have your locket?" Adam asks. "I thought it was evidence."

"I don't think Jimmy had it." I clear my throat. "I think whoever killed Jimmy did."

Amy, notebook back in hand, jots everything down.

"So where do we go from here?" Raising her head, Amy looks at us.

Before we have a chance to think, the bell rings.

"For now," Adam says with a smile. "It's back to class."

Chapter 43

"Amy? Are you OK? AMY!"

Mrs. Roth is about to shake her when Amy snaps out of it. Eager to continue the investigation following her informative lunch, Amy had been lost in thought. The rest of the class watches silently as a look of concern mixed with a hint of annoyance settles over Mrs. Roth's face.

Amy had been staring into space as ideas bounced around her head. *How will I find out where the phero-mones came from? Who had Lily's locket?*

"Sorry Mrs. Roth." Amy replies. "I'm fine."

"Good. Now maybe you would like to answer my question?" Mrs. Roth asks, not expecting an answer. "In Romeo and-"

The bell rings, signaling the end of classes for the day.

"Well I guess you're saved by the bell, so to speak." Mrs. Roth says as everyone begins packing their bags. Relief washes over Amy. She hasn't even cracked open her copy of the play yet.

"We'll pick this up tomorrow." Mrs. Roth calls to her students as they disappear into the hallway. "Come prepared!"

Amy slips out of class and enters the crowded hallway. Students rush back and forth, anxious to escape the confines of the school. She gets trapped in a traffic jam but eventually manages to squeeze past. Reaching her locker she stands close, happy to be out of the flow. She turns the lock. Right, left and then right again. After swinging her locker door open, Amy reaches into her pocket and retrieves her phone. She turns it on, taps the screen a couple times and then types a message. We have to meet NOW. Same place?

Before hitting send, Amy quickly glances up and down the hall. The swarm that had filled the hallway only moments ago has already started to thin. Nobody seems to be paying her any attention. She presses send. Amy watches the screen in anticipation, waiting for a reply. It doesn't take long. The phone vibrates and the screen lights up. Three words fill it. On my way.

After grabbing her books and shoving them into her bag, Amy slams her locker and leaves the school.

The taxi pulls to a stop. "That'll be fifteen dollars." The bearded man behind the wheel eyes Amy from the rearview mirror. "Cash or credit?"

Amy digs into her wallet and pulls out a twenty. She passes it to the man. "Keep the change."

She opens the door and escapes the stench of smoke and vomit. Once again able to breathe, Amy stands on the sidewalk and watches the cab drive away.

The Sleepeasy Motel is nestled in between two deserted industrial lots. Amy passes a tall pole with a fluorescent sign that displays the motel's name as well as pricing and availability. Fifty per night. Ten per hour. Teens, trying to be funny, have smashed the eep in Sleepeasy. The vacancy light is on.

Three cars occupy the parking lot of the two-story motel. Amy walks past the office with the word open in the window. A balding man sits behind the desk, eyes glued to a small television. A vending machine and ice box stand near the rear stairs to the second floor. Out Of Order is written on one and No Ice is written on the other. The door to the ice box is open, showing that there is indeed nothing inside.

The cement stairs are cracked and broken in various places. They could give way any day now. Taking the rusty metal railing in hand, Amy ascends. The railing shakes in her grasp. A piece of cement drops to the ground below as Amy reaches the second level.

She steps over paint chips which have fallen from the motel walls and proceeds towards her destination. A squeal of ecstasy startles Amy when she passes the second window. The drawn curtains and their flower pattern do nothing to muffle the continuing moans and groans.

Arriving at room nineteen, Amy takes a moment to survey the stained wooden door before her. Mold grows around the bottom and the number nine hangs upside down. She knocks. A bolt slides and a chain is removed. The door swings open.

"How did Lily find her locket?" Amy steps into the room and closes the door.

Chapter 44

"**H**ow many burgers do you want? Lily?"

I'm in my room examining the fading gash on my forehead when my mother calls up to me. It has started to heal but I'll probably have a scar. It could have been much worse. I pull the locket from my pocket and let it dangle in my hand. As it spins, the sunlight from my window causes it to sparkle.

"Two." I call back down while clasping the locket around my neck. Back where it belongs. I never told my mother I found it. She would probably force me to tell the police, and I can't exactly trust them.

"Hurry, before they get cold." My mother replies.

I admire the locket a few moments longer before removing it. Opening a drawer in my jewelry box, I shove it to the back.

The kitchen is empty when I enter. There is a bowl of salad sitting on the island and the sliding glass door is open. I inhale the mouthwatering aroma of cooking meat flowing through the open door. I don't know how vegetarians do it. Grabbing the bowl of salad, I let my nose lead the way onto the deck.

My mother stands next to the barbeque, metal spatula in hand, as the burgers continue to sizzle and pop. I place the salad on the table which has already been set.

Brandon is in the backyard trying to teach Zoey how to fetch. So far he seems to be failing miserably. It is quite hilarious. He tosses the tennis ball for Zoey. She chases it, picks it up and then begins rolling around. When Brandon walks towards her to retrieve the ball, Zoey quickly jumps up and moves just out of reach. He tries again to get closer and she does the same thing. I try to conceal my laughter while this continues.

"Can you pass me a plate?" My mother turns to me, hand out.

I grab the nearest dish and walk it over. After prying them free, my mother piles the finished burgers on the plate. She then arranges a couple buns on the barbeque to toast.

"Brandon! Dinner's ready!" My mother calls.

Brandon is currently rolling on the ground, trying to wrestle the ball away from Zoey. At the mention of food though, he jumps to his feet. Seeming to forget all else, he races towards the deck.

"So Lily, how are you doing?" My mother squints at my forehead. "It looks like your cut is healing nicely. I can barely tell where the stitches were."

"Yeah, it doesn't hurt anymore either." I hand her another empty plate.

"And after what happened at the hospital?" She begins filling it with the toasted buns.

"No more nightmares." I lie, not wanting her to worry.

"That's good to hear." She smiles, passes me the plate and then shuts off the barbeque. "I just can't believe the police haven't found anything."

"Yet." I say, trying to sound optimistic.

My mother and I take our seats at the table where Brandon patiently waits for his food. As soon as the buns are down, he grabs a set and digs in. Of course the large salad bowl sitting before him is totally ignored. For a few moments I watch the spectacle that is my brother. He engulfs his burger. Ketchup and mustard stream down his face. The sleeve of his shirt becomes a napkin.

"My waiting room is packed lately and there are all these reports of spider attacks. It's just hard to believe nobody has seen anything." My mother continues, breaking the trance. "There's no way a few spiders could have done that..." She pauses, looking out over the backyard. "Something has to be done! How is anyone supposed to feel safe?"

She sounds understandably frustrated and upset with the whole situation. I want to tell her about our investigation but of course I can't. The only way for us to find the truth and keep our families safe is to keep everyone else in the dark. Thankfully she decides to change the subject.

"But enough about that." She scoops some salad onto her plate while I sink my teeth into my burger. "How's Luke?"

"He's fine." I mumble with a mouthful. I finish chewing, swallow and then continue. "Spends a lot of time at home. Does a lot of painting. It's his way of taking his mind off of other things."

Since the incident at the theater, we have been taking things slow. We talk for hours on the phone and hang out at the park with Max and Zoey. I think it will be a while before we attempt another dinner date though.

"I bet." My mother brings the conversation right back to where it started. "After what he saw..." She trails off.

"Done!" Brandon leaps from his chair and bounds down the stairs towards Zoey. His face is plastered with ketchup and mustard. His plate is swimming in it. Zoey jumps up and knocks him to the ground. Brandon laughs hysterically while Zoey licks his face clean.

Turning my attention back to my mother, I notice she is staring into the distance as if lost in thought.

"Mom? Are you OK?" I wave my hand in front of her eyes. She doesn't even blink. "Mom?"

Without moving her eyes she finally replies.

"It must have been... horrible." Her eyes begin to water. "Who would want to hurt all these people?"

Chapter 45

The sun begins to set, painting the sky a vibrant pinkish red. Gladys pulls her light jacket close, shivering in the cool breeze. She ascends the front steps as quickly as her old bones will allow. The stairs creak beneath her feet. The bright porch light next to the door shines. Using the brass knocker, Gladys bangs on the door and calls out.

"Mr. Walker? Are you home?" There is no answer, so she tries again. "Vince?" The same result.

She hasn't seen him in days but heard through the grape vine that he is sick and laid up in bed. When Gladys tries knocking a third time only to receive silence, her worrying gets the better of her. She imagines Mr. Walker so sick or injured that he is unable to help himself or call out. *Maybe he fell down the stairs or maybe he asphyxiated on his own vomit.* She shudders at the thought and decides to try the door. It's unlocked.

The inside of the house is dark. She walks in and shuts the door. Fumbling in the darkness, Gladys slides her frail hands up and down the smooth wall until she finds a switch. Flicking it, the lights come on. From where she is standing the stairs to the second floor are clearly visible. There is no body at the foot of them. *So far so good*, she thinks to herself.

"Vince!"

Gladys calls out again as she finds her way into the empty kitchen. She takes a quick look around and realizes just how clean her neighbors are. Everything is spotless. No dishes in the sink, everything organized neatly on the counter, and even the towels hanging on the wall are at an even height.

Checking the other rooms on the main floor reveals the same. Spotless and empty. She decides the bedroom is her next destination and works her way back to the stairs. Grabbing the railing, she gradually inches her way to the second floor while continuing to call out. Her worry continues to rise as she repeatedly receives no answer.

When Gladys finally reaches the top she glances up and down the hallway. Unsure of which room is Mr. Walkers, she decides to start with the closest and work her way down. A washroom, a closet and a bedroom that she figures belongs to Adam. The only room left is at the end of the hall. She reaches the closed door and, bracing herself for the worst, opens it.

Empty. With the dim light that shines into the room, she can see that the bed is made and hasn't been slept in for a while. Breathing a sigh of relief, Gladys leaves the room and shuts the door. She heads back towards the stairs, intent on checking the last place in the house.

Reaching the main floor, she walks towards the back of the house and finds the door to the basement. A padlock hangs open. A sliver of light can be seen underneath. Her hand trembles as she lifts the padlock from its place and pushes the door open. A set of wooden stairs leads down to where a light bulb hangs next to a chain.

The stairs groan beneath Gladys. She makes her way down into the dimly lit room, worried they are going to give way. At the bottom, another door stands before her. Attached to the door is a large warning sign which reads: KEEP OUT!

No sign is going to tell me what to do, she thinks to herself while pulling the door open. The stench hits her before anything else. A mix of rotting meat and feces. Gladys holds her nose and presses on.

The room is brightly lit by multiple overhead lights. A couple of tables are pushed up against the wall to her right. They are covered with multiple beakers, vials, and Bunsen burners. There are narrow glass cases filled with dirt, aquariums and steel cages. All empty. A blackboard stands next to a wooden wardrobe along the opposite wall. A complicated chemical formula is scrawled across the blackboard and surrounded by numerous notes. A curtain is drawn, hiding the area near the far wall.

As Gladys walks further into the room she notices the door to the wardrobe is slightly ajar. Her curiosity takes control and she pulls the door open. It is packed to the hilt with unlabeled silver canisters and syringes. Pinned to the inside of the door are two photos. She immediately recognizes the subjects. The young girls from the football game. They are taken from a distance as if the photographer didn't want to be seen. The first photo displays one of the girls in a park with a dog at her side. The second photo shows much more skin. Wearing a black two-piece bathing suit, the other girl lays next to a pool. She has her nose in a book and seems oblivious to anything else. Two young boys stand in the background.

Gladys leans over, squinting to get a better look, when a noise from behind the curtain makes her jump. Her heart begins to race. She is about to make a run for it when the noise comes again. This time it sounds more like groaning. *It could be Vince*, she thinks to herself. *I can't leave him. What if he needs my help? That's why I'm here in the first place.*

As she moves towards the back of the room, the odor increases tremendously. It becomes so strong that holding her nose isn't doing the trick any more. Gladys gets closer. Through the curtain she can make out what looks like a bed and an arm reaching out for help.

"Vince?" Gladys is terrified, but there is no turning back now. "Is that you?"

She is reaching for the curtain when the lights go out and the laboratory door slams shut.

Chapter 46

The headlights flood the driveway as Officer Martin brings the car to life. He pulls out and turns onto the empty road.

Picking up his radio, he says into the speaker, "Well that was a bust."

He had been called out to a home on the edge of town following the report of a suspicious character dressed in black. The owners insisted they had seen this person standing outside their window, watching them. When the suspect was spotted, they apparently took off into the corn field next to the home.

The radio crackles to life. Stacy's voice comes through. "That's too bad, Hun. Whatcha going to do now?"

He smiles at the name Hun. It may not be much but he'll take what he can get.

"I guess I'll just return to the station to see your pretty face."

"My, my, Officer Martin." Stacy replies coyly. "What would your wife think?"

Officer Martin flips down the visor above his head and glances at the attached photo of his wife. "What she doesn't know won't hurt her."

They both laugh at this. Heck, their little flirtation has been going on for years and she hasn't caught on yet. So far though that's all it's been, just flirting, but Officer Martin would love to take it further. He has even fantasized about the things he would do if he had her alone. The images are playing through his mind when he notices movement in the cornfield to his right.

"What the fuck was that?" The words tumble out of his mouth before he realizes the microphone is still in hand.

"What's wrong?" Stacy crackles through.

"It's probably nothing." Officer Martin slows and then pulls the car to the side of the road. "I think I saw something. I'm going to check it out."

"Be careful, Hun."

Officer Martin returns the microphone and grabs a flashlight. Leaving the car on, he steps out and places a hand on his holster. As he walks around the front of the car, his shadow dances in the street. Standing on the other side of the car, he lifts the flashlight above his head and shines it over the field.

Corn stalks as far as the eye can see. He moves the flashlight back and forth, scanning the area. Nothing. *Maybe I just imagined it.* He starts to lower the flashlight when he sees it again. Out in the middle of the field, a few of the stalks shake and slightly bend. With his flashlight raised again he watches as the movement continues, heading in the opposite direction. *There is definitely something in there*, he realizes, *and they are trying to escape to the surrounding woods.*

"Not on my watch." He mutters under his breath.

He draws the gun from its holster and marches forward. He crosses a ditch, steps over a couple rotten logs belonging to an old wooden fence, and enters the field. He feels like he is being swallowed alive. The stalks tower over him. Numerous leaves smack him in the face as he pushes his way through.

Using the flashlight to guide his way, Officer Martin comes across a set of footprints in the dirt. With his head down and a finger resting on the trigger of his gun, he follows them one after another. As he moves further into the unknown, the set of footprints suddenly turns into two.

His heart skips a beat at the realization that he is following two people and could easily be outnumbered. The thought of calling for backup crosses his mind but he dismisses the idea until he knows exactly what he is dealing with.

The tracks lead into a small clearing where the stalks have been trampled flat. He shines his flashlight around the small area. Other than a few spider webs here and there, he doesn't notice anything. The tracks stop at the center of the circle and then head off in different directions. Officer Martin places his gun back in the holster while deciding what to do next. He begins to feel uneasy as the silence sets in. *I can't stand here all night. Just choose a set and keep moving.* He faces the footprints leading towards the woods and is about to follow them when something snaps behind him.

Chapter 47

Before Officer Martin can spin around, a burlap sack is tossed over his head. Something slams into the side of his knee. He is knocked to the ground and kicked repeatedly in the ribs. While being beaten, he can hear someone else approaching. Stalks crunch under their weight. A low hissing sound and then he is sprayed with something wet. It soaks into his shirt causing it to stick to his skin. Once he is soaked from head to toe, the hissing stops. Left damp, shivering and in pain, he listens to the crunching as both people hurry off.

As Officer Martin lies on the ground, sure that a few ribs are broken, he painfully raises a hand to his neck. A knot has been tied to hold the sack in place. He struggles with it but finally manages to untie the knot. Lifting his head ever so slightly, he slides the sack over his head and tosses it into the field.

He rolls onto his back and stares up at the stars. He takes a few deep breaths. When the pain begins to feel less intense, Officer Martin moves into a kneeling position with his good leg while keeping one hand over his ribs. The pressure seems to quench the pain. Then taking another deep breath, he pushes himself to his feet. He stumbles but catches himself.

Officer Martin checks the surrounding area and spots his flashlight shining under a few scattered leaves. Brushing them aside, he picks up the flashlight and uses it to scan the field. Near the edge of the clearing he notices the butt of a gun in the mud. He reaches down and feels his empty holster. *It must have fallen out when I was attacked.* He grabs it.

I need to get out of here. Officer Martin turns to leave. The light from the flashlight passes over the field in the direction of the woods. A couple of stalks shake. Pausing, he squints to get a better look. At first there is nothing, but then another stalk sways, and then another. Suddenly the whole field is alive. A wave that is headed straight for him. As it gets closer and closer, he feels himself raising his gun. The wave of movement reaches the clearing and stops. Officer Martin scans the field with the flashlight but doesn't see anything. That is, until he lowers the light to the ground. Black and red spiders flow out of the corn, scurrying their way towards him. He fires once, twice, even three times. They keep on coming.

He drops the gun and tries to run for the car. The pain in his leg is too much. He begins to limp, pushing his way through the corn. *Am I even going the right way?* Sweat runs down the side of his face and his chest aches.

Taking a moment to catch his breath, Officer Martin quickly turns around and shines the flashlight over the ground. It has disappeared and been replaced with a flowing carpet of black and red. They are only a few feet away now and getting closer. He continues to push on, desperate to reach the safety of his car. Officer Martin doesn't get far before he trips and lands in the mud.

He rolls onto his back in time to see the first few spiders approaching. They climb over his shoes and up the leg of his pants. He can feel their tiny feet crawling along the bare skin of his thighs. While frantically kicking his legs, he drags himself backwards. They bite the inside of his legs as he stands. Spiders drop to the ground as he violently shakes both legs.

The bites on his thighs throb as he hurries towards the road, spiders right at his heels. His spirits lift as he exits the corn field to see the light from his car. *Maybe I'll get out of this alive and see Stacy's beautiful face again.*

Reaching the fence, Officer Martin climbs over. He starts towards the car when his legs give out. *What the hell!* With no time to think about it, he drags himself towards the car. Through the ditch and onto the road. Reaching up from his place on the ground, he grabs the handle and pulls the car door open.

With arms that are weak and only getting weaker, he pulls himself across the seat and grabs the microphone. Lying on his side, he watches as the spiders scurry across the road towards the car. Trying to sit up fails. Closing the door is no longer an option. There is no feeling below his arms. Pressing the button on the microphone, he calls for help. All that comes out is a squeak. His eyes widen.

"Officer Martin?" Stacy's voice crackles through the speaker. "Is that you? What's wrong?"

He tries to reply but is unable to move his lips. Officer Martin lies frozen and helpless as the spiders near. They are about to climb inside when the dark figure appears and slams the door. Safely sealed inside the vehicle, Officer Martin thanks the heavens. He raises his eyes to the roof. The driver's side door opens while he stares at the photo of his wife.

Chapter 48

"**H**appy Halloween!"

Mrs. Davis, dressed as the greenest witch I've ever seen, flings the classroom door open. A black hat with a bent tip rests upon her head. An orange ribbon is wrapped around the base. The fake crooked nose, complete with warts, blends perfectly with her green skin. Her black gown almost reaches the floor. A pair of orange and black striped socks leads into a black pair of pointed shoes adorned with buckles.

In one hand she carries a broom and in the other a bag which she places on her desk. From inside she removes a bowl, and candy. Bags and bags of candy. She tears each bag open and empties them, one at a time, into the bowl.

"What's everyone waiting for?" Mrs. Davis looks up from the bowl and gives us all a questioning look. "Come get some."

The room erupts with cheers and laughter as everyone leaps from their seats and makes a beeline for her desk. Everyone except for Amy, Adam and I. We remain seated, once again going over our list of suspects.

Amy is convinced that, for some reason, the person behind all of this has a thing for me. She insists that I wouldn't have found my locket in Jimmy's room otherwise. I can't wrap my head around it though. No one has shown any interest in me that would also want to hurt me or my family.

"You never know." Amy raises her head from the list, "It could be someone who hasn't even spoken to you."

"I guess." I say, not really believing it.

"Will we see you guys tonight?" Eric asks us on the way back to his seat. Mounds of candy fill his hands. He places some on each of our desks.

"We'll be there." I say, ripping the wrapper off a sucker. "Thanks."

Eric and his twin brother Derek own one of the largest homes in Crescent Falls. A party is being held to celebrate one of my favorite days of the year and the whole school has been invited. I've been promised that it will be epic.

"They always go all out." Adam says, "At least that's what I hear from the people that are actually invited."

Amy and I both stick out our bottom lips.

"OK, OK. I get it. Poor Adam right?" Adam jokingly raises his arms as if to surrender. "I'll just stop talking."

"Now that everyone has had their fix," Mrs. Davis reaches a green hand into her bag and pulls out a stack of paper, "Let's get started."

We make it through class on our sugar fueled high. When the bell rings, everyone makes for the exit.

Mrs. Davis stands by the door, urging us all to take more candy for the road.

With my pockets full of sweets we head down the hallway, passing Derek along the way. While carrying a stack of flyers, he stops to chat with a group of girls. I don't hear what he says but I assume it was funny since the girls begin to giggle.

When I reach my locker, with Amy and Adam in tow, I get a good look at the flyer Derek has been passing around. It hides the lock completely. Zombies and witches cover the orange tinted page. Black block letters jump out. Eric And Derek's Ghoulish Gathering. Dedicated To The Memory Of Those We Have Lost. Friday October 31st... Obviously. 8pm Till The Break Of Dawn. You Know The Place.

I begin peeling the tape from my locker door when Derek leaves his flock of girls and heads in our direction.

"So are you guys coming tonight?" He motions towards the flyer I am currently tearing down. "Everyone's invited this year. It's times like these that we all have to stick together, right?"

"We wouldn't miss it." I finish removing the last bit of tape and hand him back his flyer.

"Great!" He looks genuinely happy to hear I will be there. "You'll get to experience your first Eric and Derek party." After a quick guilty glance at Adam and Amy he continues, "I guess you all will actually."

On that note he leaves, continuing down the hallway to the next group of students. I open my locker, exchange books and close it again. After placing them in my bag I toss it over my shoulder. Walking together, we head towards our next classes while discussing our theories and suspects.

The rest of the day flies by in an uneventful haze of sugar. It appears that getting the students full of candy is on every teacher's agenda today. With a piece of licorice hanging from my mouth, I meet Adam in the hall after my final class. We leave to meet up with Amy. She is closing her locker when we approach.

"All ready for tonight?" Adam says as he walks up behind her.

Amy nearly jumps out of her skin, before spinning around to face us.

"Sorry, didn't mean to scare you." A sly grin crosses Adam's lips. "Anyways, I figured we could all meet at my place and then go from there."

"Sounds good to me." I say as we start for the main lobby. "I just have to let Luke know to meet us there."

"Luke's coming?" Adam blurts out.

"Yeah, is that OK?" I ask.

"Yeah... Whatever... The more the merrier, right?" Adam replies, unconvincingly. We pass the main office and the mural which has recently become home to a patch of paper pumpkins.

"OK then. How about we meet around seven thirty?" I suggest.

"Fine." Adam answers.

Amy, who has been silent all this time, finally finds her voice.

"I'll be there." She says as we leave the school. "I just have to take care of something first."

Chapter 49

Only minutes from downtown, Amy pauses on the sidewalk and pulls the folded, white strip of paper from her backpack. Unfolding it, she reads the words again. 5PM. CLARA'S CAFÉ. COME ALONE.

When she opened her locker and the paper had fluttered to the floor, her heart had skipped a beat. Of course her first thought was, *who left the note?* The idea of going alone had frightened her at first. She had contemplated not going and just giving the note to the police. In the end though, her curiosity got the better of her. There was no way she was going to miss an opportunity like this. The person might have important information that she could use to her advantage. Besides, if they wanted her dead, why would they leave a note? Right?

Luckily, she was able to stuff it into her backpack before Adam and Lily had arrived at her locker. If they knew about the note, they would have insisted on tagging along. A simple "No" would not have sufficed. The last thing she would want to do is put them in danger.

Standing outside Clara's, Amy checks her phone and realizes she is early. *Might as well grab a drink and wait.*

The café is alive with the hum of chatter. Every seat in the place is occupied. Since opening, it has been the afterschool hangout for many students. Some come to study while others simply use it as a place to meet up. With fresh food and drinks at the ready it is no surprise.

The smell of fresh baked cinnamon rolls fills the air as Amy makes her way to the counter and orders her usual. Vanilla latte with extra whipped cream. She eyes the fresh rolls through the glass display case and, after some deliberation, gives in to her temptation. The young girl behind the counter passes Amy the latte and a ceramic plate which carries her cinnamon roll.

Unable to find a seat inside, Amy heads for the currently empty patio. Choosing the table furthest from the entrance, Amy sets her food down. She places her bag next to her chair, leans back with cinnamon roll in hand and takes a bite. The sweet taste of cinnamon and sugar dances over her taste buds. *This must be what heaven feels like*. Unable to control herself, she inhales the rest.

The latte washes down the roll. Whipped cream tickles her nose and coats her upper lip. The moment she begins wiping the cream away, a young boy, who couldn't be much older than ten or eleven, sprints up to her table, grabs her bag and races off.

"Hey!" Amy leaps from her chair, knocking it over in the process. "Get back here!"

The boy runs down the sidewalk and turns at the nearest corner. Amy isn't far behind. She follows him around the corner, only to see that he has dropped her bag. Amy stops to pick it up, letting the boy get further and further away. Deciding to let him go, she pulls her bag over her shoulders and walks back to the café.

After repositioning her chair, Amy sits with her bag placed snugly in her lap. She tries to relax. With everything that is in her notebook, losing it would be devastating. Her breathing begins to slow to a normal rhythm. She takes a long swig of her latte, the taste of vanilla calming her nerves. When the last drop leaves her cup, Amy checks her phone. A quarter past five and still no sign of the mystery person. *Five more minutes and then I leave. I hope I didn't miss them.*

Deciding to return the plate while she waits, Amy stands. Her world begins to spin. Feeling lightheaded, she falls back into her seat before collapsing to the ground can become reality. She blinks her increasingly heavy eyelids. Her cries for help escape as whispers. A blurry figure arrives at the table and sits across from her. She blinks once more before everything goes dark.

Chapter 50

"Come on Max." Luke calls. Standing beneath a nearby tree, Max barks at the squirrel chattering above. "Time to go."

Obedient as ever, Max bounds over to Luke's side. His leash is attached and the couple leaves the park. The squirrel continues to screech nasty things behind them.

They turn onto their street in time to watch the neighbor's porch light switch on, joining the others on the street that are already lit. *Looks like the festivities are about to begin.* Four houses down, a fairy princess, complete with tiara, skips next to her mother. One hand waves a glitter-coated wand while the other clutches a bag loaded with candy.

Max leads them up their driveway. Past the two car garage and along the pumpkin lined path towards the unlit entrance. Propped in a rocking chair, next to the front door, sits a stuffed scarecrow with a cowboy hat upon its burlap head. Luke tries the door and finds it locked. The plastic skeleton hanging from the door stares back at him with a "Better luck next time" grin.

Searching a nearby flower pot, Luke uncovers the spare key. He enters and calls out for his parents while shutting the door behind him. Once inside, Max's leash is removed. He saunters off into the house as Luke calls out again. A blue plastic bowl, filled with unopened candy packages, rests on a wooden half-moon table. Luke lifts the bowl, revealing a slip of paper. Had to go out. Be back soon. Don't scare too many little ones.

After stuffing the note in his pocket, Luke flips the switch for the porch light. He tears open the bags and pours the candy into the oversized bowl. The phone in the kitchen begins to ring. As he steps into the kitchen, the ringing suddenly ends. Luke picks up the receiver to hear nothing but silence. The line is dead. With a shrug of his shoulders, Luke returns the receiver, leaves the kitchen and heads to his room above the garage. Preparing for tonight's party is the only thing on his mind. Max sits patiently outside the closed bedroom door, waiting for Luke to reach the top of the stairs.

The door is barely open a crack when Max bursts past Luke and heads straight for the double bed. After crawling halfway under he backs out, bringing with him a half chewed bone. He then leaps onto the bed and, seemingly content, lies down with his treat. He begins to chew away.

Walking past a desk littered with sketches of multiple characters and fantastic scenery, Luke stops at the window. The fairy princess is only two houses away and getting closer. A goblin and a pirate, complete with eye patch, have now made their way onto the block as well. They both appear too old to be trick or treating.

Luke removes his shirt and drops it to the floor. Opening his closet, he digs deep until his eyes fall upon the finest shirt on the rack. While buttoning it up, Luke turns around and admires the half-finished painting currently resting on his easel. A surprise gift that he doesn't want the subject, the only girl he has ever felt the urge to paint, to know about until it is complete. He smiles at the portrait of Lily. He thinks of her and the way those few strands of hair fall perfectly over her face.

The sound of something solid hitting the floor interrupts his daydream. The separator between his bed and work space hides Max from view.

"Hey, you crazy mutt." Luke listens as Max jumps to the floor and begins knocking the bone around. "What are you doing?"

Before Luke can reach the bed, Max starts barking and darts out of the room, leaving his bone spinning in a circle on the floor. Shaking his head, Luke places his foot on the bone, stopping it in place. He realizes what all the commotion is about when the doorbell rings. Max's barking only increases when he reaches the front door.

Once downstairs, Luke learns just how flexible he can be. He holds Max back with his right foot while lifting the candy bowl in one hand and opening the door with the other. Even though his barking has ceased, the fairy princess on the other side of the door appears terrified of Max. Her mother is used as a human shield.

"It's OK. He won't bite." Luke says, placing the candy bowl back on the table. "He's just excited. Do you want to pet him?"

The little girl nods. She steps from behind her mother's legs and quickly sticks out her hand. Taking him by the collar, Luke allows Max to walk up and lick her hand. It isn't long before he moves on to her face. Luke pulls him back while the young girl simply giggles.

Luke picks up the candy bowl once again and drops some into the fairy princess' open bag.

"What do you say, Honey?" The woman asks her daughter.

"Thank you." The little girl says after watching her mother mouth the words.

"You're welcome." Luke replies. "Have a good night."

Mother and daughter are walking back down the path when the little girl turns and waves.

"Bye doggie." She calls as they continue down the driveway.

Max sits by Luke's side. He briefly watches the girl wave before barking once in her direction.

Back inside, Luke checks his cell phone. *It's that late already?* He begins typing a message to Lily, letting her know he might not be on time. Before he can finish the text, the doorbell rings again. As if on cue, Max resumes his barking routine.

"Quiet, Max." Luke says while placing his phone on the table. "It's probably just a pirate and goblin. Nothing to be afraid of."

Holding Max back, Luke opens the door to find... Nothing. The lit porch is empty. Releasing Max, Luke steps out onto the porch. He looks left and then right before spotting the teenage pirate and goblin across the street.

"I think someone's playing a trick on us, Max." Luke says while watching the couple receive another addition to their overflowing candy bags. Once the owner steps back inside, the two begin laughing amongst themselves. The goblin kicks a jack-o'-lantern into the street as they exit the driveway.

"Hey!" Luke shouts at them. Their heads whip around. When they see him, they take off running.

"Just a bunch of punks." Luke mutters.

He joins Max inside and starts to close the door. It hits something solid. Luke doesn't move quickly enough. The door is shoved in with brute force. The edge whacks him square in the face, knocking him against the wall. His face becomes flush. He feels the warmth of the blood as it leaks from his nose. It drips, leaving red spots all over the white tiled floor.

Luke pinches his nose and squints through the haze. He watches as someone dressed all in black enters his home and closes the door. Max's vicious barking breaks through the pounding in Luke's head. Max's blurry form latches onto the dark figure's leg. The dark figure feverishly shakes both their leg and the growling dog until the grip is loosened. One strong kick sends the dog sailing into the wall. Max slumps to the floor, yelping in pain.

Furious, Luke charges at the dark figure. He is knocked to the floor with one quick fist to the side of his face. Luke covers the stinging cheek with his hand while sitting up. *I have to get out of here, NOW.* Before he has a chance to move, his cell phone begins to vibrate. The dark figure watches it shake across the nearby table. It continues to vibrate as the dark figure picks it up, looks at the name of the caller and then slams the phone to the floor. Lifting their foot, they repeatedly bring their boot down on the phone, smashing it to pieces.

With the interruption dealt with, the dark figure returns their attention to Luke. They step towards him, prompting Luke to inch his way backwards into the adjoining living room. When Luke hits the back of the couch, dread sinks in. The dark figure, standing only a few feet away, reaches into their jacket and pulls out a gun. They aim it directly at Luke.

"What do you want?" Luke screams while staring at the barrel of the gun.

No reply.

"Why won't you answer me?" Luke shrieks. The dark figure only shakes their head.

A finger is placed on the trigger. The dark figure starts to pull when, as if out of nowhere, Max flies through the air. He sinks his teeth into the dark figure's arm. The gun goes off. The bullet skims Luke's ear and disappears into the back of the couch. A man's voice erupts in a painful scream from beneath the black mask. The dark figure waves his arm wildly in an attempt to shake Max free. The gun soars across the room. Blood drips from the dark figure's arm, forming a deep red pool. Frozen in a state of shock, Luke observes the dark figure twist his arm from Max's clutches.

The sound of laughter reaches the room first. The squeaking of porch steps follows. A group of trick or treaters make their way towards the door. The doorbell rings twice before the barking ensues.

Nobody moves. As the minutes pass, the group on the porch grows.

"We know you're home." The trick or treaters bang on the door, determined to gather more sugar. "We aren't leaving."

While gripping his arm, the dark figure turns to Luke. "You should have stayed away." Before retreating through the back door and into the night, he says his final words. "Her death is on you."

Chapter 51

"**I** hope they're OK."

I've been trying to reach both Luke and Amy for the past half hour now. Amy's phone goes directly to voicemail while Luke's just keeps ringing.

"I'm sure everything's fine." Adam tries to reassure me. "Maybe they're already at the party."

"Maybe..." I reply.

We sit in Adam's living room, growing tired of waiting.

"Why don't we walk over and check?" Adam suggests. "We can't wait here forever." He glances towards the staircase. "Besides, I don't really want a group of people here anyway. My dad needs his rest."

"If they do show up and we aren't here, then they will go to the party... right?" I ponder the idea. Adam nods. "OK," I say. "Let's go."

Adam turns off the lights and locks the door before becoming my GPS.

We pass groups of trick or treaters. Some are dressed in gowns while others are the things of nightmares. Watching them makes me wish I was that young again. Collecting stacks of candy and eating all I can before my mother takes it away. Stomach aches be damned.

A witch races by me. The broomstick in her hand smacks against my hip. She doesn't even notice, instead continuing to fly down the sidewalk. The vampire chasing her spreads his cape and yells, "I want to suck your blood."

When we turn onto Eric and Derek's street, I realize how big this party could be. Both sides of the road are lined with cars. Walking was obviously a good decision. Getting out of here would have been impossible.

Adam leads us towards the only house on the block where music booms and spotlights shine. A couple guys carrying a large keg approach the stream of people entering the home. The crowd parts, allowing the guys and the booze to pass.

The party is well underway. When we finally make our way inside, the first things to catch my eye are the three photos on the wall. The first is a nice shot of Jimmy in his uniform while posing on the football field. The second displays Brittney in her uniform, surrounded by the rest of her squad. The last is a rather sad picture of Nathan standing alone behind the school. There hasn't been any word on what happened to him, but after all this time I think anyone who cared has given up hope.

Following the gradually increasing sound of music, Adam and I enter the main room. There must be a fog machine somewhere. The room is filled with it. I recognize many people from school but there are also some I've never seen before. Almost every hand seems to be carrying a red plastic cup. I get the feeling some of these people started partying early.

I pick out the Snobettes on the opposite side of the room. Of course they are surrounded by a flock of young men. The girls are quite animated while talking about something pointless I'm sure. The boys appear to be listening intently but they certainly aren't watching their faces. Their heads bob up and down with the girls' every bounce.

"Let's go find the kitchen!" Adam has to shout in order for me to hear him over the music.

The entrance to the kitchen is draped in webbing. Attached to the ceiling, it hangs so low that we have to duck to get in. I feel a couple strands get caught in my hair. I work on removing them as we approach the group encircling the keg from earlier. When the person wearing the tattered and torn shirt, complete with matching pants, turns around, I realize it is Eric.

"Want a drink? It's non-alcoholic I swear." He says with a wink. Eric fills one of his red cups and holds it out to me with his rotten, zombified arm.

"Why not?" I reply, taking the cup from him. "It is a party after all."

Eric fills another cup and hands it to Adam. "Enjoy the party." Before returning to his group of friends, he adds. "And watch out for spooks."

The mediocre beer warms my throat as I follow Adam back to the main room. The walls continue to thump.

We spend some time drinking and mingling with other people from school. I ask around, but nobody has seen Amy.

After poking Adam's side, I whisper into his ear, "I'm going to try Luke again."

Attempting to find a somewhat quiet area, I step outside. The redial button is pressed and the phone on the other end rings. And rings. And rings. When I hear "You have reached", I promptly hang up. I try Amy and once again get her voicemail. Where are they?

Before I can meet back up with Adam, I'm approached by someone I've never seen. He stops me as I enter the main room. I don't recognize him from school. He actually looks a few years older than anyone else here. The bags under his bloodshot eyes tell me he hasn't slept in a while and was either crying recently or is really high. Maybe both?

"You're Lily Crawford, right?" His squeaky voice confirms my suspicions. He has definitely been crying.

"Yeah... Do I know you? I haven't seen you around. Do you go to our school?" I ask, trying to figure out who this guy is.

"No, no." He replies. "My name's Josh. I know Nathan... or knew him." His voice cracks.

"Oh... I didn't really know him." Unsure of what to say, I ask, "Were you two good friends?"

"I... We were..." His eyes begin to water. "I heard about this party and thought that maybe I would feel closer to him if I met some of his other friends." He motions around the room. "But so far I've been hard pressed to find any." He wipes a tear from the corner of his eye. "It doesn't really surprise me though. He's always been kind of an outcast." He takes a drink from his cup and then continues. "Anyways, I heard that you saw Jimmy right after... you know. How did he look? Did it look like it happened quickly? Did it look like he suffered? Did he look like he was at peace?"

My phone vibrates in my pocket while I think back on that night. The image of Jimmy's severed head still clear as day in my mind.

Not wanting to hurt Josh, especially after losing the person he obviously loved, I look him in the eyes and say, "We still don't know what happened to Nathan. We may never know. But if he is no longer with us, then he's in a better place. He can finally be at peace."

Josh nods silently and lowers his head. I pull my phone from my pocket and check the screen. It's a text from Amy. The adrenalin starts pumping as I read the short message. Found something at the falls. Hurry!

"What's there to find at the falls?" Josh asks. "I thought that place was closed down."

Realizing I read the message aloud, I shove my phone back into my pocket and give a quick shrug. "I don't know, but I have to leave. Are you going to be OK?"

"Yeah, I'll be fine." Josh places his hands on my shoulders. "Thank you, Lily."

I scan the room, searching for Adam. Vanished. When zombie Eric enters, I stop him.

"Have you seen Adam anywhere?" I ask.

"I think I just saw him heading for the wash-room." Eric says, pointing down the hall. "Why? What's up?"

"Nothing serious." I reply. "But if you see him can you tell him I had to leave?"

"Will do." He answers before returning to his cup.

To be safe, I also send Adam a text as I exit the party. Had to leave. Meeting Amy at the falls. Hopefully he isn't too upset.

There are even more cars cluttering the street than before. I hurry down the sidewalk as fast as my two feet can take me, passing a few straggling trick or treaters along the way. At least the falls aren't too far away. I try calling Amy but again get her voicemail. Maybe she can't answer her phone. My mind races. What could she have possibly found?

Before I know it, I am already over the fence and trudging through the field towards the woods and the falls beyond.

The sliver of moonlight slicing through the branches lights the tree lined path. As I follow it, the semi-darkness and silence begin to creep me out. I should be rushing but instead I slow to a crawl. I hear something rustling in the trees around me. As I inch forward, now terrified, the feeling that I'm being watched washes over me. Just keep moving. The falls are just around the next bend. The sound of water crashing against the rocks intensifies as I approach.

Before I reach the next turn, I notice movement in the trees. Suddenly someone dressed in black is standing before me on the path. I stop, frozen with fear. Over their head, a black mask covers everything except for their beady eyes. The dark figure moves towards me.

"What do you want?" I scream, dropping my phone. They move closer, unspeaking. "Who are you?"

Stopping only a few feet away, the dark figure pulls off their mask.

Chapter 52

"I'm coming, I'm coming."

Kate reaches for the remote and presses pause. The couple on screen freeze, their mouths open in mid-conversation. The banging on the door continues as Kate removes the blanket and pushes herself out of the chair. Brandon begins to stir on the couch where he passed out following an exhausting night of trick or treating with Devon. He is still clutching his bag of candy.

"What's all the banging?" Brandon says groggily while rubbing his eyes.

"Probably just some more trick or treaters." Kate replies, stepping over Zoey. The dog raises her head for a moment before going back to sleep. With the amount of visitors they have had, she is unfazed by the noise.

"I'll be right back." Kate leaves the room and enters the kitchen.

A nearly empty candy bowl sits on the island. Grabbing it, she heads towards the banging. Anxious to silence the noise, she reaches for the handle and quickly opens the door. Her thoughts of scolding the person creating the racket vanish as she is taken aback by what she sees.

Standing on the porch is none other than her daughter's boyfriend Luke. He appears to have been through the ringer, and then some. His eyes are puffy. His nose is red and swollen. Streaks of blood cover his upper lip and a fist sized bruise has begun to form along the left side of his face.

"Luke!" Kate exclaims, "What happened? Are you OK?"

He briefly explains what happened. The cut phone line, the man in black, and the gun.

"Before disappearing out the back he said her death was on me." Luke says. Kate covers her mouth, realizing the reference is probably about her daughter. "I have to find Lily."

"She's not here. She's at some party." Kate's hands begin to tremble. "What's happening? Why would someone want to hurt my baby?"

Brandon appears behind his mother, his eyes wide.

"I don't know, but I intend to find out." Luke replies before turning to leave. "Just stay inside and call the cops. Take care of Brandon, I'll find Lily."

Kate nods with tears in her eyes. She picks up her son and squeezes him tight.

While hurrying down the steps, Luke hears the door shut and the deadbolt slide into place. Reaching his car at the road side, he pulls open the door, hops behind the wheel and starts the engine. Next stop Adam Walker's.

Luke's hopes fade as he pulls up to a dark house. *I'd better check anyway.* He climbs the steps and knocks. No answer. He tries the door but it is firmly locked. Luke peeks through the windows. Nothing but dark, empty rooms. *She must have gone to the party.* Leaving the house behind, Luke hops back in the car and speeds down the road.

The street is so crowded that Luke has to park three blocks away. Two guys stumble into him as he rushes down the sidewalk.

"Watch where you're going!" They shout. Incoherent mumbling follows.

Ignoring their comments, Luke leaves them to continue their drunken rant.

Luke arrives at the house in time to witness a young woman bend over a set of rose bushes and wretch into the flower bed. With every sound she makes, the young guy holding her hair back looks like he is going to be sick himself.

"Is that... It is. Luke McKinlay!" Derek appears with his arm around a brunette. Noticing Luke's face, he stutters, "W-W-Wow man, what happened to you?"

"It's a long story Derek. Have you seen Lily Crawford?"

"Nah man. Haven't seen her." Derek looks at the woman next to him. "But I have been a little distracted." He winks at Luke. "Anyways, go on in. Get yourself a drink and party man. It looks like you need it."

On that note, Luke worms his way into the house. He immediately spots a couple making out on the stairs to the second floor. Deciding that trying to get any information from the moaning pair would be useless, he moves on. The music is pumping and the walls are shaking. It only gets louder when Luke enters the foggy, main room.

Some people are dancing while others are drinking. A couch along the wall has become another couple's makeshift bed. They round second base in plain view of everyone.

Luke tries to question people but the music is too loud. He can't hear himself, let alone anyone else. Walking to the stereo system near the front of the room, he finds and pulls the plug. The music comes to a grinding halt. Luke gets what he wanted. Everyone's attention.

Holding the plug in hand, he asks loud enough for all to hear, "Has anyone seen Lily Crawford?"

Most people reply with a shake of their head, while the others scream at him to turn the music back on. *This is hopeless... I may already be too late.* He is on the verge of plugging the system back in when Josh enters the room.

"I have."

Chapter 53

"Thank God. It's just you." As quickly as they had arrived, the tremors in my hand vanish. "Don't scare me like that." I bend over and pick up my phone. "I thought you were the killer."

Adam drops his mask to the ground and takes another step closer. "Who says I'm not?"

"Quit messing around." I offer a lighthearted laugh. "You couldn't hurt a fly."

"I guess it depends on if the fly deserved it." His teeth shine a pearly white, filling the satisfied smile.

"OK... But murder? That's just not you, Adam."

"Maybe you don't know me as well as you think you do." He takes another step forward.

"I know you couldn't do what someone did to Jimmy." I state.

"Jimmy got what was coming to him." Adam looks up as if admiring the stars. "He escaped me once, but I wasn't going to let it happen again." He takes another step closer, narrowing the gap between us. "The idea to use the football game as a diversion was genius." His smile widens when he says, "I quite enjoyed slitting his throat. The sound of gurgling blood was music to my ears." He looks at me. "Of course, it was stupid of me to be carrying your locket at the time."

I knew I shouldn't have told Amy and Adam what happened to Jimmy. "OK then, how did you get my locket?"

"And Brittney dying," Adam brings his hands together in glee. "That was just the icing on the cake."

He ignores my question. I knew he was making this all up. I continue to go along with it. "And Nathan? Is he dead?"

"I couldn't let him interfere with my experiment." Adam shrugs. "He would have ruined everything."

"Experiment?" I ask, tilting my head.

"You'll find out soon enough."

I raise my hand. "OK Adam, it's getting late." I say, checking the screen of my phone. No new messages. "You've had your fun. I have to find Amy. She asked me to meet her here."

"I know." Adam reaches into one of his jacket pockets.

"How do you know?" I ask. "Did she text you also?"

"Don't be so daft." Adam pulls out Amy's phone and holds it up for me to see. The pink faceplate is clearly visible in the moonlight. "Who do you think sent the text?"

As the glow from the phone lights the area between us, a lump begins to grow in my throat. "Adam? W-Where's Amy?" I stammer. "Is she in on this too?"

"You know... She almost left me once." He says, reminiscing about days gone by. "His name was Mark. They worked on the paper together. I got rid of that temptation. Shoved it right over the falls." Adam places the phone back in his pocket as the toothy grin disappears. "Now she's trying to leave me again?" His hands ball into fists at his side. "NOBODY LEAVES ME!"

His sudden screaming startles me. A chill rushes through me. "OK Adam, just calm down."

He relaxes his fists and reaches inside his jacket. "Now you're doing the same thing."

"It's alright, Adam." I take a step towards him, closing the gap. I place my hands on his shoulders. "We aren't going anywhere."

"Nobody leaves me." Adam repeats himself as he slides his hand from his jacket. The blade of the knife glistens in the moonlight. "Unless I release them."

Adam lunges. I raise my knee and strike my target. The knife lands in the dirt as Adam drops to the ground coughing and clutching his groin.

I dash between the trees bordering the path. A branch scrapes my arm while another slaps me across the face. Using the light from my phone to guide the way, I weave through the woods. I turn left, then right, then left again. I hear branches snap and the rustling of leaves. Adam is on the chase.

"Don't do this, Lily." He groans in the distance. "You're only making it harder on yourself."

I continue creating a maze among the trees as his calls become fainter. My breathing is heavy. I feel exhausted but I push on.

Minutes pass without a word from Adam. I stop next to a wide oak and listen. Nothing. Feeling safe for the moment, I decide to call for help. As I press nine, Adam appears and grabs my wrist from behind. He slams my hand against the tree. The phone slips from my grasp as a damp cloth is forced over my face.

Chapter **54**

I open my eyes and witness the ground hovering above me. Am I floating? Why is it moving? I shiver and realize my clothes are soaked. My shirt clings to my chest. What happened?

I remember the text from Amy. I left the party. Someone dressed in black stopped me on the path. They removed their mask. Adam!

The fog begins to clear from my mind as I take in my surroundings. The ground isn't just above me, it's all around. I realize I'm in some kind of tunnel and the ground isn't moving. I am. Lights are stationed at equal intervals along the floor, connected by what appear to be long extension cords. There is a faint humming somewhere in the distance. Is that a generator? Looking forward, I see the back of Adam's head. He holds my feet under his arms.

A drop of water lands on my forehead. I look up as another lands on my cheek. The roof of the tunnel, previously bare, is now covered in webbing. Hundreds of black and red spiders scurry over each other while I am dragged below. I clench down hard, even biting the inside of my cheek, to keep from screaming and giving myself away. I glance at Adam. He seems oblivious to the fact that I am awake.

Ouch! My shirt has risen up. Stones are scraping against my bare back. I involuntarily jerk to the side when another digs in even deeper. So much for staying low key.

When Adam stops, I quickly pull my feet back before he has a chance to tighten his grip. A forward kick hits him square in the back. He stumbles and falls to his knees while I flip myself over and bolt in the other direction. He isn't down for long. I hear splash after splash as he passes through every puddle on the tunnel floor.

I might actually get away. I might escape this nightmare. The lights go out leaving me in pitch darkness. I trip and fall, slicing my hand on the edge of a rock. The pain is excruciating but everything in me says get up and go. Back on my feet, I use the wall as a guide, sliding my good hand along it as I creep forward.

I turn a corner and the tunnel begins to brighten. In the distance, a wall of water glistens in the moonlight. The falls! We are behind the falls!

Adam tackles me from behind, knocking me to the ground. I struggle, kicking and screaming under his weight.

"Why are you doing this?" I yell while lying face first on the tunnel floor, defeated and hopeless. "What do you want?"

Without responding, Adam reaches into his pocket. As he lies on top of me, I feel something cold, thin and metallic jab into my thigh. He then stands, allowing me to roll onto my back. I spot the needle in his hand. My eyes widen.

"Don't worry. It's just something to make you a little more cooperative." Adam tosses the empty syringe aside and removes the goggles covering his eyes. They hang around his neck as he leans over me. "We wouldn't want you to try running away again would we?"

I try to kick that smug look from his face but my legs won't move. I try to raise my arms but can't even do that.

"What did you d-" My words are cut off mid-sentence. My mouth has gone numb.

"Now, now... Don't get your panties in a bunch." He chuckles to himself. "At least not yet anyway." He kneels by my side and looks into my eyes. "See, you can still breathe. You can still hear and see. It's not like your heart is going to explode in your chest or anything." Adam lifts my arm and lets it fall to the ground. "You just can't move."

I lie helpless, screaming at him in silence as he stands and then straddles my abdomen.

"And hey, if you survive then you can tell me," He pauses and taps his finger against my forehead. "What it's like to be trapped in your own body."

Standing, Adam places the goggles back over his eyes, lifts my legs and drags me back into the darkness. After a few minutes of being hauled through the stones and mud, Adam drops my legs. I'm suddenly grateful to have no feeling. I hear some movement near the side of the tunnel and suddenly the lights come back on.

Adam re-appears, his goggles hanging around his neck. He lifts my legs. "Let's continue shall we."

All I can do is stare straight ahead which, unfortunately, means I am once again looking at the ceiling. I watch as the webbing condenses and the amount of spiders above my face increases. As I am waiting for one to land on me, they begin to get farther away. The roof of the tunnel gradually slopes upwards.

Adam drags me into a brightly lit cavern. I instantly wish I was back in the tunnel. The number of spiders taking up residence here is at least triple. The ceiling is barely visible through the intricate webbing which is laced with various sized white pouches. I hope they aren't egg sacs.

Adam pulls me across the floor and drops my legs. With one quick movement he tosses me onto a filthy mattress resting next to the cave wall. With a little maneuvering, he gets me into a sitting position. What I wouldn't give to be on my back again.

The cave is massive. The tunnel we came through is on one side while another, much wider tunnel, exits through the other. The webbing extends from the ceiling all the way to the ground. I'm probably leaning against it right now! For some reason that terrifies me even more than the crimson stain which covers the majority of the cave floor.

Looking around the room, I notice even more pouches of webbing. I try to focus on the large one near me and can almost make out something inside. It looks like... a face. It is! There is someone in there, in all of them. I recognize the person as Officer Martin. I hope his death was peaceful. His eyes flick open. He stares directly at me while his lips move, mouthing the words "Help me".

There's nothing I can do. Adam steps out of sight, leaving me to watch Officer Martin repeat those same words over and over again. I hear the sound of something being dragged towards me. When Adam returns, he has someone with him. Amy! Besides being gagged and blindfolded, she doesn't look any worse for the wear. He sits her a few feet in front of me and removes the blindfold before loosening the gag and removing it from her mouth.

"Lily! Thank God! Are you OK?" Amy tries to move but rope binds her arms and legs. When I don't respond she screams at Adam, "What did you do to her?"

"She was being difficult." He answers nonchalantly. "It'll wear off eventually."

"Don't worry Lily," Amy turns back to me. "We'll get out of here. Everything will be f-"

A scraping sound erupts from deep inside the wide tunnel. The noise continues as a wave of spiders scurries forth and comes to rest on the ceiling. Amy turns her gaze towards the tunnel as the scraping gets closer.

"Well," Adam says as he pulls a knife from his pocket. "Sounds like it's dinner time."

"What do you mean?" Amy asks. "Whose dinner time? What's down there?"

Adam lets out an exasperated sigh.

"Talk, talk, talk. That's all you ever do." He shoves the gag back in Amy's mouth and ties it. "Has anyone ever told you that you ask too many questions?"

One enormous leg, coated in thin hairs, stretches into the cave. This is followed by another. And another. I don't understand how this horrifying beast is possible. I'm witnessing a spider, only one that is thousands of times larger than the others. It towers over all three of us. The hairs on its back brush against the ceiling. Multiple small spiders drop onto the hulking form. My screams echo inside my head, unable to make their way out. Amy's muffled shrieks fill the cavern for me.

Adam flips open his pocket knife and approaches the pod containing Officer Martin. He cuts a few strands and the sack falls to the ground. Then closing the knife, he places it back in his pocket and grabs the webbing with both hands. Officer Martin, his calls for help now audible, is dragged across the floor and dropped directly in the center of the crimson stain.

Like a flash, the monster strikes. Fangs sink into the sack, piercing Officer Martin's body. I have a clear view of his face and watch as his eyes slowly close. Blood flows from the webbing, pooling around it. The color fades from Officer Martin's face as the spider continues to drain him.

"So what do you think?" Adam stands next to the creature, smiling like a proud father. "Isn't she beautiful?" He runs his hand along one of its front legs. "She grew up so fast." He turns and begins talking to the spider as if it were a young child. "Now that you're this big though, there is no easy way to get you out of here. Is there?"

The spider stops feeding, briefly looks at Adam and then digs back into its meal.

"So we'll keep you here and keep you fed." Adam continues to talk to it. "And I brought you some more to eat." He motions to me and Amy. "I'll let your babies wrap them up for you."

Adam pulls a silver canister from a pocket within his jacket. While zeroing in on me, he gives the canister a quick shake. The nozzle is aimed at me and he is about to press down when something stops him. Adam releases the nozzle and places the can back in his jacket.

"You know, Lily," He looks me up and down. "You have been kind of a tease, leading me on and all." Adam unzips his jacket. "Everyone always says not to play with your food." He removes his jacket and tosses it in the corner. "But what if I play with it for them?"

Adam shoves me against the mattress and climbs on top of me. Amy screams through the gag. She tries to intervene but her hands are literally tied. Helpless to stop it, Amy simply closes her eyes and begins to hum.

When a spring in the mattress jabs me in the back, I realize whatever Adam gave me is wearing off. Because it hurt! I try to push him off and scream but I still can't move or make a sound.

Adam grinds against me while cupping my breasts through my shirt. As he squeezes them, quite hard, he presses his lips against mine and forces his tongue inside. I try to bite down. No luck. I feel him reach down. His hand slides under my shirt. Adam gradually moves his hand back up my body and, before I realize it, he is under my bra. He begins to rub my breast roughly and then grabs the nipple and sharply twists. A tear trickles down the side of my cheek. I want to scream. I want it to end. I want my mom.

To my surprise, Adam stops what he is doing and rolls off. Maybe it's all over.

"Hey, Amy!" Adam calls. She turns and glares at him. "Watch this." Adam gives Amy a smile and then turns back to me. Grabbing the bottom of my shirt he lifts it right up over my head. He then pulls out his knife and, taking hold of my bra, slices it right up the middle.

I'm left lying naked from the waist up. "Enjoy the show, Amy," Adam says. "Because you're next."

He then climbs back on top, grinding his hips hard against me. He takes my left nipple in his mouth and bites down, nearly drawing blood. My fingers twitch. Eventually he switches and sucks on the other. When Adam pushes himself up and straddles me, I hear more muffled shouts from Amy. Then I hear the sound of a zipper. Adam's hand glides along my waist and then slips inside my pants.

"Get away from her!" Luke's voice echoes through the cave.

Startled, Adam leaps off of me. While doing up his pants, he slowly backs out of sight.

My mouth opens. I manage to stutter, "L-L-Luke."

"It's going to be OK, Lily." Luke, gun in hand, steps into view. "I'm here now."

While keeping the gun aimed at its target, Luke helps to cover me. With my motor skills gradually returning, I'm able to assist.

"Y-Your face." I stammer, taking notice of the damage.

"It'll be alright." Luke replies while returning me to a sitting position.

Adam stands silently in line with Luke's gun. Where did he get a gun? The web covered body of Officer Martin still rests in the middle of the room surrounded by a puddle of blood. The spider is nowhere to be seen. As Luke leans over to remove the gag from Amy's mouth, we hear the scraping again.

Amy screams through the gag.

I manage, "W-Watch out!"

Before I know it the giant spider has entered the room. Luke backs up, stumbles, and falls to the ground. The gun slips from his hand and slides across the cavern floor, coming to a stop at my feet. The creature spots Luke and prepares to strike. As it rears its head, I grab the gun in my shaking hands, aim and fire.

"Noooo!" Adam leaps in front of the giant spider before falling to the ground, unmoving.

I close my eyes and continue to pull the trigger. The cave fills with the ringing of shot after shot after shot.

Chapter 55

Sirens continue to wail as the squad car pulls to a stop near the emergency entrance. The ambulance ahead of us swings open its doors. Adam remains unconscious as the paramedics wheel him and his stretcher into the hospital. Luke, Amy and I step out of the car and through the sliding glass doors. My mother meets me in tears. I can't hold back anymore. They flow out of me too. With my body back in my control, I latch onto her, never wanting to let go. What went down in that cave was horrible. As much as I would like to, it was an experience I'll never forget.

Adam is rushed into surgery where the doctors plan to remove the bullet that hit him. Part of me hopes he dies on the operating table. Most of me actually. He certainly deserves it.

We are gathered in the crowded waiting room when Amy's parents arrive. She races into their open arms. They briefly wave in our direction before leading, an eager to leave, Amy away. The glass doors slide shut behind them.

Minutes pass and names are called. I watch the clock on the wall tick past the three and then the six. After an hour, our number is up.

"Lucas McKinlay?" A nurse appears with a clipboard in hand.

Luke stands and follows her. As he exits the waiting room, he passes a man with short dark hair.

"Daddy!" I shout, momentarily forgetting the other people occupying the room. He joins us, settling into the empty seat next to me.

"I came as soon as I heard." He takes my hand in his. "How are you Princess?"

I pull my hand away and wrap my arms around my father. I offer a weak smile. "I've been better."

My parents are doing their best to lighten the mood and take my mind off of recent events when a couple of gossiping nurses pass the waiting room.

"Did you hear we have a killer in our midst?"

"Really? Where?" The other asks, excitement in her voice.

"He was in surgery but now they've got him in a private room. There's guards and everything." Her voice becomes deep and eerie. "Stay out of the east wing if you want to live."

Their laughter slowly diminishes as they get farther away. The need to speak to Adam overwhelms me. I have to find out why he did what he did.

"Could you both maybe get me something from the cafeteria?" I rub my stomach. "I'm getting really hungry."

"Why don't you come with us?" My father suggests.

"I want to be here when Luke comes back." It's not a complete lie. Looking at my father, I say, "Plus, it'll give you guys some time to talk."

My mother chimes in. "We don't want to leave you al-"

"I'll be fine." I provide them with my best version of puppy dog eyes. "Pleeease?"

Reluctantly they agree. As soon as they're out of sight, I bolt.

The room is easy to find. The only one with a guard stationed outside. As I approach, the door opens.

"Lily," Chief Wright steps out of Adam's room with his jacket over his shoulder. He stops me in the hall. "You shouldn't be here."

"I need to talk to him. I have to." I motion to the uniformed officer. "Besides, he'll be here to protect me. What's the worst that could happen?"

Chief Wright seems to think it over and then nods. "OK, but only for a few minutes."

He begins to slip on his jacket when I notice the bandages covering his right arm. "What happened?" I ask, pointing to the wound. "Are you OK?"

"Oh, it's nothing." He pulls the sleeve of his jacket over the bandages while focusing on something behind me. Turning, I see Luke step towards the nurse's station at the opposite end of the hall. Damn, he's finished already? As Chief Wright watches Luke he says, "Let's just say I'll be more careful when taking out the trash from now on."

He smiles and I smile back. Maybe he's starting to relax a bit where I'm concerned. Trying not to be seen by Luke, I thank Chief Wright and slip into the room.

Adam lies in a hospital bed with his left hand cuffed to the side. Various wires crawl out of his gown and trail towards monitors that continue to beep in rhythm. He looks exhausted, but I'm not about to let him sleep. When he spots me, he turns his head away.

"What do you want?" Adam asks, his voice weak.

"Why would you... No. How could you do this?" I march over to the side of the bed and grab his arm. I just want to shake him until the beeping from the monitors stops. "Murdering innocent people? Children? Torturing your friends?"

Adam looks me straight in the eye and then gives a slight shrug as if it means absolutely nothing. All he says is, "She had to eat."

His answer shocks me. I thought we had been friends. How could I not have seen how messed up Adam is?

When I don't reply, Adam sits up in his bed and says, "And you got what you deserved. Although you deserved worse after the way you treated me." He pauses to catch his breath. "Leaving me for that guy."

"His name is Luke." I reply, not about to give in to his pity party. "And we were never really together. Never. I was just trying to help you. That's it."

"Whatever." He says lying back down.

Trying to get his mind off of Luke I ask, "What about that creature?" I shudder just picturing it. That monster could have eaten us alive. I can only imagine what would have happened if it had gotten loose. "How did it get so large?"

"Oh, you mean my baby girl?" Adam questions sarcastically. "The one you murdered?"

"It would have killed us all!" I blurt out, starting to get a little frustrated.

"Well maybe it should have." Adam retorts.

It takes everything in me to stand my ground and not strangle him right then and there. I count to ten and take a deep breath. We glare at each other for a moment before he relents.

"Science runs in the family." He laughs to himself. "I was working on something that would make me strong enough to keep people from bothering me. Sure there are steroids, but I wanted something fast and untraceable." He repositions himself in the bed. "It was working on my test subject. A couple drops mixed with his morning coffee did wonders." A glass of water sits next to his bed. He downs it all. "We had a lab at home with insects and plants of all sorts. One day I thought, what would happen if I give it to them?" He pauses as if trying to build suspense. I wish he would just spit it out. "Maybe I used too much. I'm not really sure. All I know is it worked!" Adam is beaming now as if this is something to be proud of. "The only problem is that it worked too well. They just kept growing. I had to set them free."

One word catches my attention. "What do you mean them?"

Totally ignoring my question he continues, "So I brought my baby to the cave where I thought she would be safe. That's where I had another idea." He begins coughing, the amount of talking taking its toll on him. Once it is finally under control he says, "Maybe I didn't have to use it on myself. Maybe I could let the others deal with people for me."

"That's horrible!" My mind returns to the cave and I remember the goggles around Adam's neck, the lighting along the tunnel and the generator powering everything. "How did you do all this alone?" I ask. "You must have had help."

"And I have you to thank for that." He replies. "If you hadn't pointed out that my mother was pregnant in her wedding photo, I never would have thought to dig. Old photos do reveal so much."

"What are you saying?"

"Let's just say that I put two and two together and realized I was lied to my whole life. Not that it was Vince's fault. He was as in the dark as I was." Adam answers, cryptic as ever. "When I confronted my real father, he confirmed everything. Then when dear old Dad found out what I was up to, he was more than willing to help."

"Who?" I demand an answer. "Who is your father?"

All I receive is a shake of the head and a tight lip. I'm done.

"WHO IS YOUR FATHER?" I shout at him. "WHAT DO YOU MEAN OTHERS? WHERE IS MR. WALKER?"

The corner of his mouth curls up in a sly grin. Adam takes a quick glance around the room and then motions for me to get closer. I lean over the bed, placing my ear as close to him as I'm willing to get.

The door bursts open as Adam whispers, "Someday I'll finish what I started in that cave."

Chapter 56

Leaves crunch beneath the wheels as Laura pushes the stroller through the grass. She watches the blue cotton top of Noah's bucket hat as he bounces up and down, rocking the stroller back and forth. The rocking intensifies as the playground gets closer.

"Park, Mommy!" Noah exclaims with joy. His little hand reaches from the stroller, pointing.

"That's right." Laura replies, proud of her little boy.

A cool breeze causes Laura to shiver ever so slightly. She pulls her jacket closer and tightens the scarf around her neck. *There won't be many park days left*, she thinks to herself. *Not without being bundled to the max.*

Other than a young girl on the slide, the playground is deserted. A woman with long dark hair sits on a wooden bench, watching the girl from over a newspaper. Steering the stroller in her direction, Laura parks it next to the bench and takes a seat.

Before Laura can say anything to the woman beside her, Noah shouts, "Look, Mommy!" He points at the girl at the bottom of the slide. "Sarah!"

"Yes, it's Sarah." Laura replies as she reaches into the stroller and lifts him out. "Want to go play?"

His eyes light up as he enthusiastically nods his head up and down. Laura zips his little red jacket to the top. When his belly pops out from below, she pulls down his shirt and the bottom of his jacket to cover it. She tries to re-adjust his hat but Noah covers his head with both hands. The cartoon polar bear peeks between his fingers.

"Mine!" He yells, acting like she was about to steal his most prized possession.

"OK." Laura laughs, holding her hands up. "It's yours." She gives him a soft pat on the bottom. "Go play."

He runs as fast as his little legs can take him and joins Sarah on the playground.

"Thanks for coming, Crystal." Laura turns, finally getting a chance to acknowledge her longtime friend. She motions to the kids. "He enjoys playing with Sarah. Maybe it's because she's older." Laura laughs at the thought.

"No problem. I needed to get out of the house anyway." Crystal replies.

"What are you reading?" Laura points to the folded newspaper now resting on the bench. "Anything interesting?"

"It's an article my daughter wrote." Crystal passes the paper to Laura.

"How is Amy doing..." Laura pauses, unsure of how to continue. "After everything?"

"She's actually doing a lot better." Crystal watches the children chase each other through the sand beneath the playground. "I think writing about it helps."

"I heard the trial starts next week." Laura unfolds the paper and reads the headline: Terror Beneath The Falls by Amy Vail.

"Yeah, and apparently they still haven't found Chief Wright." Crystal replies, anger creeping into her voice. "I hope they find him and they both fry for what they did."

Laura nods in agreement. "At least it will all be over soon."

After a good twenty minute game of tag, Sarah becomes bored and suggests building a castle. Both children plop down in the sand. As the walls come together, they decide something else is needed. Following Sarah's guidance, Noah uses his hand to dig a surrounding trench. When an ant begins to approach, Noah giggles and drops a handful of dirt, burying it alive. He watches as the mound shifts and grains fall. Eventually the ant crawls out and scurries away. It isn't until the trench is nearly complete that he has to swat away two more.

"Well, I think it's time we get going." Crystal says. "Dinner won't cook itself." She calls to her daughter. "Sarah, time to go."

"But Mom," Sarah calls back, pretending to pout. "We're not done our castle."

"You will see Noah again." Crystal walks over and observes their masterpiece. "You can work on your castle another day."

"Fine." Sarah says. Then turning to Noah, "Keep working and we'll finish it later, OK?"

"OK, Sarah." Noah replies.

After saying their goodbyes, Crystal and Sarah leave the park. Noah continues to wave until they are out of sight. When he returns to digging, Noah finds the trench has filled to the brim with ants. He swats at those closest before grabbing handful after handful and crushing them in his hands. As the amount continues to grow, he calls out, "Mommy!"

Laura remains on the park bench, her face behind Crystal's paper. The article about Adam Walker is enticing and she is determined to finish reading it. Without so much as a glance in his direction, she calls back to her son, "Just a minute, Noah."

Back in the sand, the number of ants swarming Noah has tripled. He attempts to stand. The ground shifts, knocking him back down. It gives way and he starts to sink. Before Noah has a chance to scream, he is gone. The only thing that remains is his hat, half buried beneath the sand.

"Alright Noah, what did you want?" Laura finishes the article, folds the paper and places it at her side. She looks to where her son was, only minutes ago, and sees nothing. "Noah?" Laura calls out to him while stepping towards the collapsed castle in the sand. She scans the area and notices his hat poking out of the dirt. Reaching down, she picks it up and dusts grains of sand from the orange octopus logo.

"Come on, Noah." Laura calls, starting to get worried. "This is no time for games."

She circles the playground, frantically searching for her son. She checks within the yellow plastic tunnel before climbing to the top of the playground for a better view. Nothing. Panic takes hold. Laura starts back towards the stroller and her cell phone. As she crosses the grass, the pain in her chest brings her to her knees.

Gripping the hat in her hands, she screams one last time. "NOAH!"

Chris Sheehan lives in Southwestern Ontario. For more information about the author and upcoming books, visit www.ChrisSheehan.ca